I0618678

Ruling Tagawoogah

Stephanie Webster

© 2020 Lulu Author. All rights reserved.
ISBN 978-1-67810-045-2

Introduction

Ruling Tagawoogah tells of the adventures, trials, and joys of the Noble Six during the one hundred years that they ruled Tagawoogah. The events chronicled here take place between the books Tagawoogah and Feud in Tagawoogah.

A strange world where animals speak..where the Great Master walks with man..where mystery and danger await around every corner...

The Noble Six--Dick, Joanna, Meg Sarah, Lucus, Juliet, and Davy--have been brought to the land of Tagawoogah by a strange force. They have defeated the Black Knight and the evil Witch in the First Battle with the help of the Taganian creatures and the panther Shelton, once King of Tagawoogah. The Great Master has blessed the Six and made it very clear that Richard is His choice for the next king of Tagawoogah. However, the Noble Six are far from being ready to rule the land. As the story begins, the Six have been living an easy life with Shelton in the Royal Mansion, but Shelton has sent them to finish their training in the Great Wood with a wise Teacher.

Part One--Rulers in Training

One misty morning in a land far, far away, six people plodded through the forest behind a strange creature. The creature, an emna, was walking quickly, but stopping often to allow his followers to catch up with him. His eyes darted back and forth and he flicked his tail impatiently, his long, hairy fingers occasionally resting on the sword at his side. Anyone familiar with the emna of Tagawoogah could tell that this one was nervous, but the six humans following the creature appeared not to notice.

The Six were young; they could hardly be called more than children in their world. The eldest was Richard, commonly called "Dick" or "Dicken". He was a handsome young man with his dark hair and black eyes and good-natured face. It could easily be told from the lad's broad shoulders and the sureness of his stride that Dicken had the makings of a fine man. The second was a girl, Joanna by name. She was "Jo" or "Josey" to her siblings. Joanna was a thin, slight girl of fourteen with hair and eyes that matched Dick's. The two youngest, Juliet and Davy, followed closely behind Joanna. Meg Sarah followed behind them, and Lucus brought up the rear. Meg Sarah was the second girl at twelve. She had pale skin and thin, light-blonde hair with sparkling green eyes. Lucus was ten, though the husky, blonde, blue-eyed lad could easily have passed for fifteen.

"Can we not stop for a rest?" Joanna loudly inquired of the Emna. "The little ones are tired." Joanna was the motherly one of the Six, always looking out for her younger siblings.

 "Ay, let us stop," six-year-old Davy hollered to the emna. "We have been walking for hours." The youngest of the Six plopped down on a nearby log, and the others followed his lead. The emna reluctantly joined them.

"The house of The Teacher is not far. If we only keep going quickly, we will reach it by high noon, methinks," the emna said. Eight-year-old Juliet, who was a sensitive girl and a peacemaker, spoke to the emna. "Prithee tell us of this Teacher," she said gently. "What is he like? What sort of things will he teach us of?"

The emna seemed to relax slightly as he answered the little girl. "The Teacher is old, but respected of all. He is very wise and very good. He was trained by the Master Himself and did spend some time in the world from which you came, so that he knows much of the sons of man. He will teach thee many things, child." The creature studied all the children, who were looking at him. "He will teach all of you to be Taganian Masters. He will train you in all types of combat, how to handle the sword and bow. He will teach you to hunt and survive in the wilderness. And he will teach you the ways and laws of Tagawoogah and of the Great Book. Whenst you have finished the training, you will return prepared to take Shelton's place and rule Tagawoogah."

"We already know these things that you speak of," Lucus said with a wave of his hand. "This must have been the most stupid thing Shelton has thought of-- to send us to this so-said Teacher. We do not need to be trained more. I am ready to rule now, and I do not understand why we must go stay with this Teacher out in the middle of Timbuktu."

"Patience," the emna said. He rose. "Let us now be on our way."

"Cheer up, Lucus," Joanna told her younger brother as the children once more started after the emna. "The training will not be difficult, nor should it last long." Joanna did not know how wrong she would prove to be.

The sun was going down by the time the seven travelers reached the clearing where The Teacher lived. A tiny hut made of mud and twigs stood under a tree. Otherwise there was nothing in the clearing. The emna rang a little bell above the door of the hut and shuffled his feet as he waited nervously. The six children put down their bundles and flopped onto the ground, some sitting, others sprawled on the grass. Suddenly the children and the emna were startled by a loud, shrill voice behind them. "Up, up, young ones! What think, that sitting on the ground is a good thing to do when visiting others?!" The voice carried a note of authority, and the children all scrambled up and turned to see who was speaking to them. It was Zattu, the famous Teacher. At first the Six did not see him, then Joanna spotted the creature and pointed him out to the others. Zattu was a little creature, about the size of a koala bear. He had bright little black eyes, like beads, in his furry round face. His fur was a smoky gray; his big ears round like those of a mouse. His tail was long and furry and black, and he flicked the end of it while he studied the Six. The Williams children looked at the little creature with surprise. This is the great Teacher we heard so much about ? Lucus thought. What can he teach us?

"It cannot be Zattu," Dick whispered. But the emna hurried forward and bowed respectfully before the little creature, who was perched on a stump so he could see better. "Great Teacher," the emna began. But before the emna could finish his prepared speech, Zattu began to ask questions of him. "Who are you? Why have you come? Who are these young ones?"

"I am Sheta, an emna. I am a trusted servant in the Royal Mansion. The Great Shelton, King of Tagawoogah, has sent me here with these young ones. They are to be trained and then sent back to Shelton to become the next rulers of this Great Land."

"Well," said Zattu with a snort, studying the Six. "If'n the Shelton want-es me to make the next rulers of Tagawoogah, he will have to send me better material." He thumped his tail against the stump, as if to emphasize his words.

The Six looked at each other. The emna made a sound somewhat resembling a nervous chuckle. "These are the best, good master," he ventured. "These are the Noble Six. They were chosen of the Great Master Himself, they were. They--"

"Noble Six?" repeated Zattu. "Noble Six, indeed! Humph! Poppycock! These Six be but weak and spoiled children who have been living in the Royal Mansion and been waited on hand and foot for many moons. They have not done anything at all worth speaking of."

Dick bit his lip to keep from protesting the creature's speech. He was not used to being talked about this way. The creatures had always respected and obeyed him and his siblings for the simple reason that they were the Noble Six. This was different, and he did not like it. But if there was one thing that Shelton had taught him and his siblings, it was to be respectful to authority and not talk back to one with a higher station and even to be very careful to not speak badly to one of lower station unless it was needed. A Taganian's name and station were all he had. In Tagawoogah only a king owned land or property of any kind. But how dare Zattu speak so, Dick thought. We have done much worth speaking of. We delivered this land and these past months we have not been behaved foolishly, but have been in training with our master, the good Shelton. We have learned the customs of Tagawoogah and how to rule and have studied the language and writing of Tagawoogah in the Temple of the Great One. Why, Zattu would be dead if it weren't for us!

Lucus was thinking similar thoughts. The Teacher is such a little creature. I could wring his neck without half a bother, and should with his speaking so to us. How dare he? Lucus scowled at Zattu.

Zattu shook his head at the children. He looked right at Dick, as if reading his thoughts. "Ay, and if it were not for Shelton and the Great Master, you Six should not be in the Great Land." He turned back to the Emna. "Much to learn, they have. Much. And though I were the best teacher in Tagawoogah, I cannot make much out of these flimsy Six."

"Flimsy!" exclaimed Meg Sarah then, who had so far controlled her hot temper. "We may look weak, but we are not, I assure you! We can do anything that you want us to. We can show you that!" The other five nodded their heads, agreeing with their sister. Zattu ignored the girl and turned to the emna. "Bring the children back to your master who sent you. I will have nothing to do with them. I cannot train them."

"Please reconsider, great Teacher," begged Sheta. "The King of Tagawoogah asks you to train these Six. The Great Master would not have it any other way. You are to be their trainer." Zattu flicked his tail and made a growling noise in his throat. He would not budge.

"Well, then, what is the matter with them, pray tell?" asked Sheta, making still another effort to convince the stubborn creature to agree to train the children.

"What is wrong!? What is wrong!?" repeated Zattu. "Just look at them!"

Sheta looked at the children, then back at Zattu with a look of bewilderment.

Zattu made an impatient tssk sound in his throat. "They are all too proud, yet very weak," said he. "They have a willingness to learn, but many be the faults that plague them! If'n Shelton had half a brain in his skull, he would have curbed these faults instead of encouraging them." He looked first at Dicken. "This one is Rikkas, a Warrior. But his mind dwelleth oft on his own matters and not on those of his Master." Dick opened his mouth to protest, but Zattu was speaking again. "And this one," he said, indicating Joanna, "She is Joannas, the One-Who-Struggles. Her hand and tongue are against everyone continually. She counteth up the faults of her brother and bindeth them about her neck. She is like a fielv in that she listens to nothing and no one. This dost not become a woman. The second girl is Jetta, the Arrow. Verily, she is like an arrow; she flieth quickly and with little thought, only sometime striking her target. Her temper is as an hot fire that cannot be quenched. Lucus is Barak-San, the Son of Lightning. He beeth like lightning that strikes without warning. In his heart is much scheming. Who can know this one?" He shook his head and made a tssk noise. "No good, no good. I see no good in them. What am I to do if'n I have naught good to work with?"

"What about us?" Juliet asked. She turned her sweet face to look at Zattu. "You forgot Davy and me." The little girl's freckled round face and begging eyes did not seem to soften the heart of Zattu. "Hmmph," said he, studying Juliet and Davy. "You two have many fears, little ones. Fears of darkness, fears of pain, fears of the unknown. Whilst the older four are arrogant and independent, you two rely too much on others."

"You must take them, I pray thee," Sheta begged Zattu. "I must carry out my orders. Do what you can with them."
"No," snapped Zattu, his tail thumping the stump. "I will not say it anon. I feel strongly on the matter."

"Do take them, Zattu," a soft voice said. All was silent as the eight turned to look at the owner of the voice. A black jaguar padded into the clearing. The cat walked lightly, almost noiselessly, on her huge paws. Her black fur was smooth and clean, her green eyes gentle. She sat down between Zattu and the Six.

Zattu spoke to the cat. "Loketa, my best, why dost thou say so?"
"It was once thought that nothing good would come of me," the big cat said. "Do take the little ones, my master." Zattu made a snuffling noise as he looked at his favorite student. The little creature appeared to be thinking deeply, then he said gravely, "Very well. As the cat hath spoken, so will I do. I will take the young ones and do what can be done. I promise nothing. The Great One alone knows if mine training will do them any good. They are of earth." The creature turned away.

The emna lost no time in thanking Zattu and taking his leave. He appeared to be quite relieved, his face the face of one who had just lost a great burden. Once Sheta had gone, Zattu turned to the Six. "To sleep, young ones," he said gruffly. "Training begins tomorrow."

"Sleep?" Davy repeated. "It is not our bedtime."
"Now 'tis," said Zattu, as he turned to leave. "Rise early you shall."
"Won't you show us our beds?" Juliet asked, looking doubtfully at the tiny hut.   "Your beds you will make," Zattu said.
"What!?" exclaimed Lucus.
"Your beds you will make," Zattu repeated patiently. "None of you may enter my hut unless I give word."
Zattu and Loketa went into the hut and closed the door.

The Six looked at each other for a moment, then Dick shrugged, and everyone began gathering brush and spreading blankets on the ground to make places to sleep. For several months they had lived a comfortable life in the royal mansion. Each one had his own room and bed. Servants waited on them. No one forced them to do anything. Shelton was usually too busy to pay them much mind, so the Six did whatever they wanted every day. Their studies they did not complete unless they felt like it. Some days they did not study with the scribes in the Temple at all. This was a different story altogether, and they were not all sure they liked it.

"Well, it is nice to sleep under the stars," Joanna said, trying to make light of the present situation.

"We are not altogether strangers to sleeping outdoors," Dick reminded the others. "We did it while traveling to the Valley of Nepeon."
"It seems like that was forever ago," Juliet said.
"Yeah," agreed Lucus. "The ground seems harder than it was then."
"And I don't remember all the strange noises," added Davy.

Joanna chuckled. "You probably were too tired to hear or feel anything. You just went to sleep."
"You guys will have to get used to more than hard ground and strange noises, you know, if we are to successfully complete this training as we promised Shelton," said Dick.
"How did Zattu know all about us by just looking at us?" Joanna wondered aloud. "It's like he read our minds. Methinks there is more to this creature than we know."

The next morning, the children were awakened early by Zattu's sharp claws in the back. "Up, up!" he called as he went to each of the Six.

"Time now 'tis to start the training!"

"Ugh," grumbled Lucus, stretching. "Thanks, Zattu," he said with sarcasm. "My back didn't already hurt from sleeping on the ground."
Juliet yelped. "Zattu, it is not morning. The sun is not up."
"Ah, but 'tis morn," Zattu said. He had with him a sack of corn and some large, flat stones. "Grind and shuck this corn," he commanded the Six. "No ground corn, no break-fast."

And so the training began. Soon the Six learned to get by with two scanty meals a day, a few hours' sleep at night, and only a little bit of shelter, for that is what they got for the years they trained with Zattu in the Great Wood. The training program began with long weeks of strenuous exercise. Under Zattu's critical eye, the Noble Six ran laps around 'the track', climbed trees, swam for long periods in moving, icy water; walked tightropes, practiced hand-to-hand combat, and navigated Zattu's 'obstacle course' which consisted of jumps and tunnels. Zattu urged them to push themselves to the utmost limit. "Faster, faster!" he would call. "Do not stop now. Rulers must be strong in body as well as in soul and mind. Step it up, Juliet. Rulers must be ready for anything. Step lightly, Rikkas, softly like a Taganian. Barak-San, keep your balance. Always keep your balance. Feet apart and shoulders back. Chin down, Joannas."

Zattu also taught the children about the Master and the Great Book and the history of Tagawoogah. He taught them how to walk, talk, and act like a Taganian. In one exercise, Zattu taught the children to be careful to never show emotion. "Men's thoughts are most plainly writ on his face," he would tell them time and time again. "Betray you, your feelings shall. Keep these things inside, you must. Trust in the Master. Do not show on thy face what thy heart feeleth. Never cry out whenst ill news hast reached thine ear. Keep thy face still. Emotions are a man's greatest weakness. Ay, keep thy face still even as a Taganian doeth. Verily, in quietness and in confidence shall your strength be."

Zattu instructed the children how to live their lives. "Praise not thyself, young ones," he told them, "neither seek gold nor silver nor jewels. Only live thy life in all humbleness and honesty, and thou shalt have the praise of many, and much treasure beside. In thine own eyes, do not see thyself as wise. Pride goeth before utter destruction, and a haughty spirit before certain fall.

"Swear not by the heavens, for they are the throne of the Great One; nor by the Earth, for it is His footstool. In fact, never swear at all. Let thy 'nay' be always nay and thy 'ay' always true. Do not be greedy for more. Verily, one in the hand is worth two in the bush." He taught them to be persistent and confident in themselves. When one of the children would complain during a difficult exercise, Zattu would punish the culprit. If one of them said, "Zattu, I'm trying, but I just can't do this," Zattu would punish him and scold. He would say, "Nay, child, never try!" Always do!" Never seek! Always find!"

One night when the day's training was over and the six children and two creatures rested by the fire, Dick asked Zattu, "Good Teacher, what must I trust? May I trust my heart to guide me?"

"No," Zattu replied. "Only a fool trusteth in his own heart. The heart of man is deceitful above all things and most desperately wicked. None can know the ways of the heart."

"Then what must I trust?" Dick asked softly.

"Trust the Master," replied Zattu. "Always trust the Master."

Zattu taught the children how to use the Binding Force to communicate with each other and with the Master. He showed them many things concerning the Force, but encouraged them to learn more by themselves. "There is naught else I can teach you concerning the Binding Force," he told them one day. "Time wilt strengthen the bond. Many knowings of the Force you wilt only learn on your own, young ones. There is none who can teach you more." Zattu also urged the children to find their "giftings". These gifts had been given to each of the Six on the day they had given their lives to the Great One. Juliet's gift was the gift of encouragement. Juliet could coax her siblings out of their bad moods and move them to work together. She could convince them to do their very best and pick them up when they felt down. If anyone was feeling upset, Juliet was the one to call. If there were negotiations to make, Juliet was the one to call. Juliet was the caring one, the nurse. Juliet's Taganinan name meant "She-Who-Comes-Beside", and Juliet was indeed the one who always came alongside to help and encourage.

Meg Sarah was given the gift of healing. She spent hours in the woods with Loketa and other creatures, learning about plants which were used for medicines. Meg Sarah could wrap broken bones so that they could heal properly, cure all kinds of diseases, and treat bruises, cuts, and burns.

Dicken had the gift of prophecy. He could understand and piece together great mysteries and puzzles, and very often felt when something was wrong or out of place, and sometimes could even foretell future events.

Davy's was the gift of history. Davy was the one who could easily recall past events and would sit for hours hearing the creatures of Tagawoogah tell stories of their history. The boy could often see the past and was sometimes called upon to recount a past event and tell when it occurred.

Lucus had the gift of written language. He, in fact, was the only one of the Six who finished the language studies at the temple. He was often called upon to translate or write when something had to be put down into words.

Joanna became upset when she saw her other siblings discovering and using their gifts, for she could not find hers. She expressed her frustration to Zattu over this. "Master Zattu, I cannot tell mine gift. The matter troubleth me. I must yet have a gifting." Zattu make a tssk noise in his throat. "Patience, Joannas. The One-Who-Struggles must be patient now. Yes, yes. Child, thy gift will come," Zattu assured her. "You have it. You need only to find it. In time you will find it. Others may only find theirs sooner. Yours will come."

Zattu and Loketa took the Six on a journey through the Great Wood. They showed the children all the creatures and told them of their habits. They showed them which plants were good for eating and which were "healing herbs". They taught them how to survive in the wilderness and how to defend themselves against snakes, spiders, and other harmful things.

One day, Zattu called the children to stand before them. He looked each of them up and down for a long moment, then he sent for a small colony of melves to make new clothes for the Noble Six. The clothes they were wearing were by now quite worn out. The melves of Tagawoogah were the very best at making clothes. The little creatures came and measured the six children from head to toe with their paws, chittering to each other the whole time. Then they scurried away and returned in a few days with the clothes. The girls were taken off in one direction by one group of melves and the boys in another. The melves busied themselves dressing the children, then stepped back to admire their work, twitching their tails happily. The six children looked at their new clothes, then at each other. They were all dressed the same--dressed as a young Taganian warrior. The outfit consisted of tight black leggings with a thin, long-sleeved brown cotton shirt. Over this, they wore a sleeveless leather jacket called a hanbirk. The hanbirk was also brown and hung halfway to the knees. On their feet they wore moccasins made of soft doeskin and decorated with tiny shells. Over one shoulder was tied a brown, folded cloak. It was to be always carried about for use as a bandage, a blanket, or as extra clothing, for mornings and nights in Tagawoogah were rather cool. Around the waist, a thick belt was tied, with a sheath on either side--one for the sword and another, smaller one, for a knife.

In time the Six completed their training. Their skin became very brown from the sun and wind and their bodies were very healthy from the fresh air and Taganian herbs. They became strong and agile, as they were accustomed to running and jumping and wrestling and swimming for hours every day. The palms of their hands and the soles of their feet were hard from climbing trees and walking barefoot. They had all become very skilled with the sword and very fluent in the Taganian tongue. There was now a confidence in their stance and a sureness in their walk and a quickness in their eyes that had not been there before.

Zattu summoned Sheta. The Emna was many days in coming, but when he finally came and was standing before Zattu, Zattu presented the Six to him. The Emna looked surprised at the great change that had come over the Six. These strong, brown, surefooted warriors were nothing like the weak and complaining children he had escorted from the Royal Mansion five years before.   "Take the younglings," Zattu instructed Sheta. "Tell your master, King Shelton, that they have finished their training. There is no more I can do with them."

Upon their return to the Royal Mansion, the Noble Six found that the King Shelton and many of the land's creatures had already begun a crowning celebration for them. Shelton lost no time in having Dick crowned King Richard of Tagawoogah. Shelton appeared relieved as he blessed the Noble Six and took his leave. It is not certain where Shelton went after the crowning ceremony, but he was never seen again. It is said by some that he went back to the Forbidden Country. Others say he left this world and went to the Kingdom of the Great One.

And so Dick became king. With as much dignity as he could muster, the sixteen-year-old boy stood before the assembly of creatures and claimed his kingdom. Dicken gave a short speech to the Taganian creatures, reminding them briefly of their history and promising to be a good king.

"As my first act of office, I will call forward my brothers and sisters," he said. The rest of the Six came and stood on the platform beside Dick, and their older brother assigned them duties before the whole crowd of creatures. Lucus was given the position of High Sheriff of Tagawoogah. Lucus was also Second-King, which meant that if something happened to Dick, Lucus would be in charge. Joanna and Meg Sarah were appointed Royal Advisors to the king. Joanna and Juliet were put in charge of foreign relations and defense, and Meg Sarah was the Supervisor of the Treasury and the Royal Mansion. Juliet, who was artistic, was put in charge of the Palace Grounds and the interior of the Royal Mansion. Davy was the Head Keeper of Records and the Deputy-Sheriff.

For the first few years of Dicken's reign, the Six busied themselves with settling in to the Royal Mansion, hunting, exploring the land, and with their many duties. Every day, creatures came to speak to King Richard, some only curious and wanting to see everything for themselves, and others with problems or complaints. Lucus and Davy were often sent here and there to settle land disputes, supervise the building of dams, or, on occasion, to bring a troublemaker to King Richard to be dealt with in court. Joanna raised up an army of creatures to be ready to aid their king if needed and supervised their training and making of weapons. She also found two great male lions, the strongest in the land, and assigned them to be Dick's bodyguards. Meg Sarah supervised the housekeepers and maids to make sure the interior of the mansion was kept clean, and she appointed a huge, sleek black jaguar to guard the mansion and grounds. Juliet oversaw the planting and keeping of the flower gardens around the Mansion and the palace grounds and saw to it that gardeners were found to keep the gardens beautiful. Juliet also spent a great deal of time on artwork and decorations for the Mansion. The Six spent much of their free time exploring Tagawoogah. Sometimes a group of two or three or maybe all six of them would be away from the Mansion for months, pressing further into unknown territory. They took long hunting trips into the Stag-deer Land and hunted herese dragons in the Country of Hills. Soon all of Tagawoogah had been mapped by the Noble Six--something that had never been done before. Meg Sarah studied all the plants and animals of Tagawoogah and wrote detailed essays on them.

On one of these exploring trips, Joanna came upon a wolf's den in the woods that had been abandoned for some time. She examined it and was about to move on when a feeble whine was heard from deep inside. Surprised, Joanna moved in for a closer look and found four tiny wolf cubs that had been left by their mother when her pack had moved on. Three of them were dead, but the fourth, a skinny, sorry-looking male pup, was still barely alive. Joanna, who always had a soft spot for animals, especially baby animals, brought the little creature home and raised him herself. Soon he grew to be a huge male wolf with long silky black fur. He was named Jeshka ,and he guarded the Royal Mansion faithfully for many years. When he was fully grown, Joanna found a suitable mate for him and Jeshka sired many more fine pups. Many years later, it would be a descendant of Jeshka that followed Joanna into battle.

Squinting against the sun, Joanna leaned against the fence and watched the horse trotting at the end of his long lead rope. One of her responsibilities that she particularly enjoyed was choosing suitable mounts for the army. Every horse in the royal stables had been hand-picked by Joanna, and she prided herself in this. The Noble Six and their army had the best horses in Tagawoogah.

She motioned to the handler, who urged the horse into a gallop.

"He won't do," Joanna said, speaking to the stable-hand at her side. "He is strong, but see how his neck is too short? This, and his stocky build together show he is not a good long-distance runner. See also his legs, how short they are. He is never going to make a good jumper. His gait is also uneven; he leads with the wrong foot."

She motioned to the handler again, who brought the horse to a walk, then finally a halt in front of the girl.

Joanna climbed the fence to the inside of the paddock. She approached the stallion quietly and began to run her fingers over him expertly. She checked his legs, his feet. His teeth. She measured him. Only slightly over 14 hands. She thought he looked too short. She backed away and motioned to the handler to take him around the ring once more.

"Such beautiful color, though," she said. "I have not seen such a perfect paint in many a year. And so gentle. He behaves perfectly. Did you see how he lifted his feet and opened his mouth for me? Such good manners. He won't do for the army, but I will mention him at supper. I happen to know that Davy is looking for a nice quiet pacer for the trails. He will do beautifully."

Part Two—The Escape from Spar-ion

Joanna rose very early, before the rest of the royal household, as was her habit. Moving carefully in the semi-darkness of her room, she found her hanbirk and pulled it on over her shirt and leggings and tied her cloak over her shoulder. Next, she slid her feet into soft moccasins and started off, moving quietly as to not wake those still sleeping. After a quick stop in the kitchen to grab something to eat to hold her over until break-fast, Joanna slipped outside. This was the day. The day the Noble Six were going to navigate the Saka--the Great Water. All six of the Williams were excited for this adventure and the question of what lay beyond the Saka had been a much-discussed topic among them for years. Now they would finally find out. Though the prospect of expanding their exploring career had appealed to everyone, it had been Dicken who had suggested this journey across the Saka. Joanna had expressed some doubts about the trip, sure. Not because she liked adventure any less than the others. No. But she did voice what they were putting themselves up against. They were exploring unknown territory. Any number of things could happen. Many dangers lurked in the Saka, and no doubt, beyond. They could get lost and never get back to Tagawoogah... But now Joanna would not think of all this. They had discussed it and were going anyway. And they were going today. Everything was ready. The boys had built a large raft and tested it until even Joanna had to admit it was sound and waterproof. Meg Sarah and Juliet had gathered enough supplies to last them for quite a while. The creatures had not understood the need to leave Tagawoogah and find out what lay beyond. Some feared their beloved leaders had gone mad. Many firmly believed the Noble Six would never return from their dangerous quest; even though Dick tried to convince them otherwise.

Joanna smiled to herself as she remembered the looks and comments of the large group of creatures who had assembled to watch Dick and Lucus construct the raft. The scene reminded her of Noah and the ark. None of the creatures would be coming along today, she knew. It was going to be only the six Williams. Skimming through the dewy grass, Joanna moved toward the stream near the Mansion. She dipped her hands in the cool water and washed her face. As she cleaned the marks of sleep from around her eyes, Joanna began going over in her mind all the things that she needed to do before they left.

"Joannas."

Though it had been years since her training, the voice of her former teacher immediately brought Joanna to her feet, standing at attention. It was an act done almost without thought.

Zattu stood under a mulberry tree at the edge of the wood. Joanna smiled, pleased to see the little creature again. Zattu never had made the trip to the Royal Mansion. What now had brought him all this way? Joanna was curious, but she greeted Zattu respectfully.

"Master Zattu. It maketh my heart warm to see thee, and so well beside. By mine sooth, age has done well upon thee."

But Zattu only snuffled and lashed his tail and scowled at Joanna. "I come not to give ear to trivialties," he huffed. "Mine business concerneth thy brother's fool errand."

"Ah," said Joanna. "Then you have heard."

"Heard!?" repeated Zattu impatiently. "All of Tagawoogah has heard of this accursed voyage upon the Saka, and I come now to speak reason into thy senseless head."

Joanna appeared unmoved. "Then you do not approve."

"Approve!?" cried the latter, stomping his foot. "Ye all be such stupid creatures! Knew I not this whenst I trained thee in the Great Wood?"

"You must speak to mine brother then," Joanna said.

"Nay," Zattu said, the mention of Dick's name seeming to suddenly quiet him. "To the mansion have I come, albet I wilt not see the face of Master Richard anon. 'Tis not meet for me to see the king."

"Then I wilt assuredly speak thy words into his ears myself," Joanna said. Zattu turned and took his leave. Joanna watched him go. When Zattu had vanished into the forest, Joanna went back to the Mansion.

The royal Mansion was a hubbub of activity as everyone bustled about, preparing for the journey. Joanna almost ran right into Juliet, who was pushing a broom. "Ach!" Juliet said. "Watch thy place, sister. Meg Sarah hath ordered the mansion to be cleaned so 'twil be in order when we come back."

"If'n we ever come back," Joanna muttered under her breath as she went on her way.

She soon saw Meg Sarah, who was hauling some boxes toward the door. "Luke! I have more boxes for you to carry down to the raft!" she called.

Davy was dusting some furniture nearby. He turned and rolled his eyes. "By mine sooth, there will be no room left for us whenst Meg Sarah is through," he told Joanna.

Joanna chuckled a little and continued on her way to the throne-room to find Dick. The doors to the great hall were closed and the two lions who guarded the way to the throne-room were on high alert, as always.

Joanna pulled one of the doors open a crack and slipped inside. The great hall was beautiful. Joanna always liked this part of the mansion best. The floor was polished marble and the walls an earthen color covered with designs and decorated with paintings. The trail of animal skins in the middle of the floor led to the throne. Above the entrance to the throneroom was the map of Tagawoogah. Two more lions crouched near the throne, but rose when they saw Joanna.

"Dicken?" Joanna's voice echoed in the empty hall.

Master Richard emerged from behind the curtains that surrounded his chamber.

"Joanna," he greeted his sister. "I was about to take my leave. Walk with me." He snapped his fingers, and immediately the two lions rose to follow their king.

"Zattu came," Joanna said as the two walked side-by-side.

"Ay," Dicken said, as if this were no surprise for him.

"He doth not approve of the journey," Joanna said. "He thinks us fools."

"Then let him think it," Dick said. "I care not."

"You will not listen to his words then?" Joanna inquired.

"I listened to Zattu long enough," Dick replied. "I am his student no longer. His words have no bearing here."

"Mmm," murmured Joanna. Dick did have a point. Their training was done. They were to make their own decisions.

Dicken glanced sideways at his sister. "You see truth in the words of the Teacher." It was more of a statement than a question.

"I don't know, Dick," Joanna ventured. "Mayhap this is a bad idea."

Richard stopped and turned to face her. "You can stay, you know. You do not have to come with us."

Joanna was silent for a bit, then spoke firmly. "Nigh, but I wilt come. We Six must alway stay together. I must help you look after the others. I cannot let you go without me."

Despite Joanna's misgivings concerning the journey, she found herself catching some of the excitement of her siblings as they finished last-minute preparations and piled onto the raft. Dick, Davy, and Lucus used long poles to push them out to sea. Joanna slipped her arm around Juliet as they watched the shores of Tagawoogah fading into the distance. The journey had begun.

The first few days on the raft were rather pleasant. The weather was nice and the water calm. During the day, the Six entertained themselves with the things they had brought-- Meg Sarah, the doctor and scientist, with her books and her papers and navigational instruments; Juliet, the artist, with her drawings, Joanna with her stories and poems, Dick with making and sharpening of weapons. Lucus and Davy tried fishing.

At night there would be singing and storytelling and they would lay and look up at the stars.

But by the fifth day of navigating the Saka, everyone was ready to be off the raft. Tempers ran short and words were said that should not have been said. Everyone became more and more impatient as the hours ticked slowly by with still no sign of land. The water stretched on and on, as far as the eye could see. To add to their problems, the weather turned very warm and sultry and the fish seemed to vanish.

"Oh for a bit of breeze," Juliet sighed, pulling her sticky hair back from her damp forehead.

Joanna wiped some sweat off her upper lip with her sleeve. "Ay. 'Twould make it more bearable."

Davy and Lucus looked on sullenly. The six had all removed their hanbirks and rolled their long sleeves up to their shoulders. Their leggings they had rolled up past their knees. The boys wore only their leggings. Their bare skin glistened with sweat. Joanna wished that the girls had the luxury of removing their shirts as well.

Meg Sarah was pacing the raft, and each time she got to one end, Joanna worried she would fall in. The raft was definitely not designed for pacing.

"We must be getting farther away from land. Or maybe close to land? We must be somewhere. The water has not changed. It is still the same salty seawater. There is not a living thing in the water. The air has become warmer--"

"Yeah, no kidding," muttered Lucus.

Meg Sarah plopped down on the side of the raft and dangled her feet in the water. "What does this mean?" She ran a hand over her forehead.

Suddenly Meg let out a scream. The other five immediately rushed to her aid.

"Sharks!" hollered Lucus. "Get the weapons!"

The sharks were driven away, but it was too late. The damage had been done. A large chunk of flesh had been torn from Meg Sarah's leg.

Though Meg was the healer, she never had been good at being the patient. She screamed and struggled and lashed out at her siblings as if she had suddenly gone mad. It took all three boys to hold her down so that Joanna and Juliet could clean and bandage the wound.

Master Richard sat cross-legged in a corner. Darkness had begun to fall and all was silent. The waters of the Saka gently rocked the raft. It was almost soothing after the hectic events of the day.

Joanna came quietly and sat next to Dick. She could not read his face in the semi-darkness, and she wondered what he was thinking. Was Dick feeling guilty for bringing them along on this perilous quest into dangerous waters? Was he considering turning back, now that Meg Sarah was injured?

"How is Meg Sarah?" Dick inquired.

"She finally fell asleep," Joanna answered. "Juliet has offered to sit up with her for a few hours."

Dick nodded; but said nothing.

"Dicken, we are running out of drinking water. We are going to have to ration it."

"Then ration it."

His voice was harsh, and it startled Joanna, who stared at him for a minute, then quietly stood.

"Ay, Master," she murmured.

Later that night, tragedy struck yet again in the form of a fierce storm. The wind blew violently against the raft and tossed it to and fro until the Six were left holding on for dear life as gigantic waves crashed over their heads and lightning lit up the night sky. In the morning, the storm was over, and Joanna began to count heads. Thankfully they had not lost anyone. At least, not yet...

But when Joanna checked Meg Sarah's wound, she was alarmed and called for Dicken.

"Dick," she said softly, "You have to look. I cannot tell for sure, but I think it is blood poisoning."

At first Meg Sarah refused to let Dick look at her leg, but she finally consented.

"'Tis as you feared," Dick said gravely as he looked. "Blood poisoning."

Meg Sarah was feverish and drifted in and out of consciousness for the next few days. Joanna and Juliet fussed over her at all hours, but they soon had to admit there was not much they could do for their sister. "She needs antibiotics," Joanna said in frustration. "And her wound needs to be flushed. But we have no water to spare. I don't know what to do except apply herbs and honey."

"Don't look at me," Lucus said. "Do I look like a doctor?"

Joanna groaned. "No, Lucus. You just were the closest person to complain to."

On the fourth day after the storm, Davy and Lucus watched as Juliet dripped the last of the drinking water between Meg Sarah's cracked lips.

"We're all gonna die," Lucus told Davy solemnly.

Juliet sighed and reached to brush a stray lock of hair from Meg Sarah's flushed face. Most likely the boys were right. The raft had been driven off course by the storm, leaving them very lost. Now it was impossible to turn around and find their way back without Meg Sarah's navigational skills. Not that turning back would do anyone any good. They would die of thirst before they reached Tagawoogah. No, the only thing left to do was hold on, and hope and pray that they would find land soon.

Joanna sat watching her wounded sister's chest rise and fall. Without water, Meg Sarah would die soon. That is, if the infection did not kill her first. Master, help us. Do you not care if we all perish? Are we not Your chosen ones? Joanna pressed her fingers to her throbbing temples. How much longer would she be forced to watch as her sister grew weaker and weaker? How long until death claimed all of them?

Davy lay on his stomach on the rough boards of the raft, too weak to move. Too weak to care if he did move. The hot sun beat down upon him, but he did not join Lucus and Dicken under the little bit of shelter the lean-to offered. He had not had a drop of water in two days and nights, but he felt as if he had been missing this daily essential for an eternity. There was a little food left, but Joanna and Dick had insisted that they save it. Davy forced himself to open his heavy eyes. He squinted against the sun, searching for the sight of-—

"Land." At first it was only a hoarse whisper, then it was a joyful cry. "Land! Land! Land ho!" hollered Davy. Instantly everyone emerged from the shelter to join their brother.

"Land!" echoed Juliet. "We are saved!"

Upon reaching shore, it was decided that whoever had the strength would go with Dick to locate fresh water while everyone else would stay with Meg Sarah. Joanna was the weakest, as she had been staying up nights with Meg Sarah and had not gotten much sleep for days. She had also been secretly giving most of her daily food ration to her younger siblings.

Davy, being the youngest, found that the lack of water and the effects of the hot sun had been harder on him than on the others. So Dick, Juliet, and Lucus were to find water and bring some back for the others. As they ate the rest of the food and packed their bags with canteens, Juliet leaned close to speak in Davy's ear.

"What will we find in this strange land, Davy? Will our mission be successful?"

Davy shook his head and sighed. "I see the past, not the future, sister."

So the three set out, not knowing where they were or where they were going, but making their way along best as they could. Dick made a map of sorts as they went, so they could easily find their way back to the others. Soon the Six would learn that the land they had found was the land of Spar-ion and the very dirt they treaded upon had been dedicated to Abaddon, the Evil One.

"'Tis but a dry, barren wasteland," Juliet observed aloud. "Nothing here but hot sand and hills and more hot sand and hills. Of a surety there is no water here."

Dick kept walking. "There is water. I saw an lizard. All living things must have water."

"I see nothing here," Juliet said. "And methinks lizards drink out of cactus or something, right, Lucus?"

Lucus squinted against the hot sun. "I know not, sister," he panted, "Albet if you see an cactus, I will be the first to attempt to extract water therein." Lucus raised his voice to call to Dicken, who was in the lead. "We must needs spread out. We could cover more ground."

"Well spoken," agreed Dick. "Fan out, but keep within hearing distance," he instructed Lucus and Juliet.

It was Lucus who stumbled upon the remains of an ancient Spar-ion temple. Stone steps led underground. Upon descending, Lucus found himself in a large room. A small diamond resting on a table in the center caught his eye. Lucus made his way forward cautiously to inspect the stone. The jewel sparkled and lit up the middle of the room. On the outside it was bright and beautiful, but inside it was black and bleak. Lucus stared at the diamond, fascinated. How could anything so bright and lovely on the outside be so very dark and foreboding inside? he wondered. In fact, the inside of the crystal grew darker and darker the more one gazed upon it. The darkness inside the gem told Lucus to leave, to avert his eyes. It silently warned him to flee while he still could. But the brightness on the outside called to him. Lucus, Lucus. Lucus knew he should leave, but still the shining surface beckoned him. Lucus, Lucus. He reached out a hand to touch the stone.

"Luke!"

Lucus jerked his hand back as if he had just touched a hot object. He whirled around. It was Dicken.

"Forsooth, Lucus, the Good Book saith, 'touch not the unclean thing'," Dick quoted.

"But look at it, Dicken!" protested Lucus. "Have you ever seen the like?"

"'Tis a crystal ball of a sort," replied Dick, turning away. "Come. Let us leave this accursed place."

Dicken left, but before following him, Lucus took the stone and slipped it into his pocket.

When Lucus emerged from underground, he heard Juliet's call of "Water! Dicken, Lucus, I found water!"

The lad hurried toward Juliet's voice as fast as his weary body would allow. Cresting a hill, he saw Juliet and Dick in a pool of water below, drinking like horses with their faces in the water. "Thank the Great One," Lucus murmured. He scrambled down to collapse beside them. Lucus began to gulp in the water greedily. He ducked his head under to cool his dusty forehead and neck. Dick was completely in the water now, and Juliet was filling canteens as fast as she could. "Hurry, Lucus!" she said, "You are the fastest, so run and bring these to Jo-—"

Juliet's voice died on her lips as she looked up at the hill. Lucus followed her gaze. His heart sank. Covering the hill and surrounding the pool were over fifty armed Spar-ion warriors.

"I don't trust them," Joanna said. Joanna and her brothers were walking about a Spar-ion village. The village was inside a large fortress made of rock and well-guarded.

"Come, Josey," Dick said, stopping to examine some wares for sale inside a booth. "You worry too much. The Spar-ions have been kind to us. The chief gives us food and drink and lets us stay in the palace. And Meg Sarah is recovering nicely under the care of the chief's doctors."

"Ay, she recovers," Joanna agreed grudgingly. "Albet what if they only care for Meg Sarah to earn our trust so as they can kill us? Assuredly they have liers in wait upon our lives, ready to throttle us in our sleep."

"Nay," Dicken replied. "If'n they meant to murder us, why would they treat us so well?"

"They are strange creatures, the Spar-ions," Davy remarked. "So like men, they are. 'Tis eerie."

"Ay," agreed Lucus, going the long way around a bunch of the creatures who were sitting in a circle weaving baskets.

"I wonder if they know about Tagawoogah," Dick said aloud.

"Better they not know," Joanna said. She shivered. "I have a bad feeling about this place, Dicken."

Joanna pushed aside the curtain that separated Meg Sarah's chamber from her own.

"How is she?" she asked Juliet.

"Sleeping. I have not let her out of my sight, just like you said," Juliet assured Joanna. "And I have examined everything the doctors brought for her before allowing them to do anything, just like you told me."

Joanna knelt beside the bed next to Juliet. "Good. She looks better, methinks."

"Ay," Juliet said softly. "She becometh stronger every day. To-day she walked the room a bit, leaning on my shoulder."

The two girls watched their sleeping sister in silence. Then Juliet whispered, "Joanna, I feel uneasy here. The Spar-ion creatures hath the evil eye."

"I know, Juliet," Joanna said, hugging her sister. "Albet do not be afraid. I am certain Dicken would not have us stay here if there were any real danger. And I am sure we will leave as soon as Meg is well."

Actually, Joanna was not sure of either, but at least she hoped so.

Juliet chuckled. "As always, you are right, Joannas. Assuredly, I know not why I whisper. I forget that the Spar-ions cannot understand us, though we can understand them."

Joanna squeezed her sister's hand.

Joanna arose early the next morning, and after checking on Meg Sarah, she went outside the palace. Dick met her. "How is Meg Sarah?" he questioned.

"She is well," Joanna answered. "Davy is with her. I daren't let her alone with those doctors."

"They are all leaving. Come look!" Lucus called from where he stood by the wall. Joanna went over to join her younger brother. Together, they watched as all the Spar-ions marched in a line out of the city. "Where are they going?" she wondered aloud.

"'Tis their Sabbath," Dick said from behind them. "They go down to their temples."

"Probably to ask the Evil One's blessing upon our deaths," muttered Joanna.

"Ah. Have the whole place to ourselves," Lucus said.

Joanna turned to Dicken. "Now's our chance. We must get Meg Sarah and make a break for it."

Dicken scowled.

"And I guess that's a no," Joanna said with a sigh. "I'm going to find something to eat."

It was almost dusk by the time the Spar-ions returned to the city. A large banquet was prepared in the palace. Though Joanna, Davy, Juliet, and Lucus had their food delivered to Meg Sarah's chamber and ate there, Dick joined the Spar-ion chief and his servants in the great hall. He excused himself early and went to join his siblings, but he found only Juliet with Meg Sarah. "They all decided to go to bed early," Juliet said when Dick inquired of their whereabouts.

"Prithee let me sit with her awhile," Dick said. "You look tired." Juliet gratefully took her leave.

A few hours later, Meg Sarah awoke and asked for water, and Dick left her chamber to go fetch her some. He filled a canteen in the water pool outside and was about to go back when he heard a shuffling in the darkness and decided to investigate.

Two figures stood together whispering in the shadows of the courtyard. It was the Spar-ion chief and his son.

"It is the full moon," the chief was saying, "We have the blessings of Lucifer. In the morning we will kill the men from across the Saka. Give the word, Abbisha. Seal up the palace. None shall escape."

Dick slipped noiselessly to Lucus's chamber. "Lucus," he whispered loudly, shaking his brother awake. "Fetch Davy and come to Meg Sarah's chamber. I will get the girls. Hurry! The natives seek to kill us." Lucus jumped up and began pulling on his clothes.

Soon the Six were gathered together around Meg Sarah's bed. Joanna brought with her bundles of supplies she had gathered. "Good on you, Josey," Dick said approvingly, eying the bundles.

"Hmmph," Joanna said. "I have been hoarding supplies for our flight since we got here."

"Guys!" hissed Juliet. "Now is not the time! We need to figure out how we are going to get out of here without being seen."

"No worries," said Lucus. "There is an underground passage that leads out of the city. The entrance is in the great hall. I did some exploring to-day whenst the Spar-ions were at the temple."

"Well done, Lucus," Dicken said.

"Ay, good on you, Luke," echoed Joanna.

Now was Lucus's turn to hmmph. "You underestimate me. I have been looking out for our route of escape since we got here."

So Lucus lead the way, sword drawn. Joanna followed with her crossbow and Dick came behind, carrying Meg Sarah. Davy and Juliet came last.

They were able to avoid most of the guards, but the guards at the entrance to the great hall had to be dispatched. Joanna stood lookout while Lucus helped the others into the tunnel.

"Joanna, quickly!" Lucus whispered.

Joanna hurried to join the others, and Lucus closed the door behind them.

"You are sure about this, right, Lucus?" Dick asked his younger brother who was leading the way with a torch held aloft.

"Of course," Lucus said. "Have you any reason to doubt me?"

"That's questionable," Juliet muttered.

"We always seem to find ourselves in damp, dark, smelly places," Meg Sarah observed.

"Dick's fault," Joanna said.

"My fault?" Dick protested. "Why is it my fault?"

"Shhh," Lucus whispered. "We are almost to the end."

Joanna did not know how they made it back to their raft in the dark, but somehow they did. But no sooner had they reached the shoreline than they heard a great noise behind them and saw a multitude of Spar-ions coming at a fast pace, armed with torches and spears.

"Quickly, now," Dicken said. "Out and under."

So they pushed the raft out a way and then ducked underwater, clinging to the bottom of the raft. The seconds dragged by. It seemed an eternity before Dicken gave them the signal that it was safe to come up. The other five dragged themselves, gasping, onto the raft. Dick had grabbed an oar and was pushing them toward open water as fast as he could. "Hurry! They may be back." Lucus and Davy grabbed oars and began helping him. Joanna crawled over to her sisters. "Are you all right?" she asked anxiously.

"We're fine," Meg Sarah assured her. "Now to find my navigational charts--—"

Part Three---The Iovis Revolt

With Meg Sarah's help, the Six made it safely back to the shores of Tagawoogah. But all was not well in the land they had left.

"There is a great stirring among the Iovis." Joanna said as she stood before Dick's throne, giving him the report.

Dick rolled his eyes. "When, pray tell, is there not a stir amongst the Iovis?"

"This time it is a threat, Dicken, I fear," said Joanna. "They said we would never come back and so have chosen a king to sit on the throne of Richard and rule Tagawoogah. Verily, 'tis a rebellion and must needs be dealt with most speedily."

"A rebellion?" repeated Dick. "Nay, 'tis no great matter, little sister. I will send Davy with peace and goodwill to assure the lovis that we are back safely, and the rightful king is upon the throne. Then shalt they put away their foolish imaginations and all will go on as before."

"Should not someone go with Davy?" Joanna asked, looking doubtful. "Forsooth, this be an dangerous errand. The lovis be not of mind for peaceful negotiations," she said.

Dick waved her away. "Bring Davy to me, sister, so I can send him in my name. All shall be well. You will see."

Joanna picked at her food. "It has been four days, and still Davy has not returned from among the lovis. He should have been back by now, else sent word."

"Lucus," said Meg Sarah, "Have you heard from Davy?"

"Not I," said Lucus. "Am I now my brother's keeper?"

"No," Meg Sarah said. "I just thought that if any of us received a message from Davy, it would be you."

"'Tis not unlike our Davy to wander off," Dick said. "He hath a free spirit. Leave him be, Joanna. Mayhap he hath been occupied with other things."

Joanna rose from the table. "He is in trouble, Dicken! Did I not tell you not to send him alone!?"

Dick continued eating. "I do not think him unwell. Surely he hath his own reasons to tarry."

"Then you will not speak against my going to find him," Joanna said.

"I will come with you," said Meg Sarah, rising from the table.

Dick sighed. "Josey-—"

"Rider on the ridge! Rider, ho!" The call of a watchman on the wall caused everyone at the table to look up.

"There, see. There he is now," Dick said.

But Joanna was already halfway to the door.

She paused only long enough to recognize his brown-and-white horse, then ran out to meet Davy. But as she approached, Joanna realized that something was wrong. The horse was missing its saddle, and, instead of sitting up straight, Davy slumped against the horse's neck. "Davy!" she cried. "Guys, help! Davy's hurt!"

She reached her youngest brother and ran her fingers over him, her heart pounding. Oh Master, let there be a pulse. Let him be alive...O Master, if there be any grace, any mercy given to me, let it now be given to him....

Davy appeared unconscious and his face was white, but he was breathing. Joanna sighed in relief, then drew in her breath sharply when she saw the gash on Davy's head.

The others appeared and helped Joanna ease Davy off his horse's back.

Meg Sarah took charge of the situation. "Bring him to my chamber.

Gently, now." She spoke quietly to Juliet. "I need hot water and rags and my bag." Once Davy had been safely deposited on her bed, Meg Sarah shooed Lucus, Dick, and Joanna from the room.

It seemed to Joanna that they waited hours outside Meg Sarah's chamber while Juliet and Meg Sarah worked on Davy. Finally Meg Sarah appeared. They all looked up.

"Well?" Dick asked. "How is he?"

"He has a gash in his forehead, but it fortunately did not go very deep. I was able to stitch it up nicely and I am quite pleased with the results. He lost a lot of blood, though, and he is sure to have a whopper of a headache when he wakes up. He has some broken ribs that will take some time to heal. His right leg is broken, but the bone fortunately did not pierce the skin. I have set it, and I believe he wilt make a full recovery. There is a small puncture wound in his foot that I will be watching for infection. He was lucky. I have the feeling that it could have been much worse."

"The Iovis?" questioned Lucus.

Meg Sarah nodded. "The cut was clean."

"A sword?" Dick murmured.

Meg Sarah pursed her lips. "Looks like it."

Two days later Davy stood before Dick in the court and gave him his report. "They ambushed me. A group of Iovis. They saw me coming. I barely escaped with my life."

"'Tis war, then," Dick said gravely. He turned to Joanna. "Sound the trumpet. Call all my troops to arms. This very day we ride."

The revolt was limited to only a small pocket of lovis in the Great Wood, and the rebellion was quickly put down. But no sooner had Dick and Joanna returned from pursuing the lovis in the Great Wood that a fielv flew in, crying, "Boats! Many, many boats! Boats on the Saka! They are approaching the west border!"

"Show me," Dick commanded the bird, kicking his horse. Joanna and Lucus followed suit, and the three galloped toward the western border, the fielv in the lead.

"What is it, Dicken?" Joanna asked, peering from the bushes.

Dick muttered something unintelligible.

"Dick, what is it?" Joanna repeated, more urgently.

Lucus spoke for Dicken. "The Spar-ions."

"The Spar-ions?! How could they have found us? What meaneth it?" gasped Joanna.

Dick shook his head. He did not take his eyes from the boats as he spoke quietly to Lucus. "Summon the troops and have them standing by." Lucus slipped away.

Dick emerged from the bushes and stood on shore to meet the first boat. Joanna followed.

One Spar-ion warrior stepped out of the lead boat and waded through the shallow water to the shore.

"Alack, the chief sends a messenger to speak to thee," Joanna said quietly.

The Spar-ion came and stood before Dick.

"Why have you breached our borders?" Dick demanded harshly.

"You have stolen the token of our people," the messenger said.

Dick's eyes flashed. "We have done no such thing."

"The chief sayeth, 'Give us what is ours and we will spare your lives'," the messenger said.

"We do not have this symbol. Thou seekest trouble where there is none," Dicken said, crossing his arms.

"What shall I tell my master who sent me?" inquired the messenger.

"Tell him I have an army here, waiting on my command. Tell him to turn about and return in peace to Spar-ion while there is yet time."

Dick and Joanna waited while the Spar-ion went and spoke to the others in the boat and then returned. "The chief will not leave."

"So be it then," said Dicken, drawing his sword. "If they refuse to leave, they will die."

Meg Sarah, who had been staying at the Royal Mansion with Juliet and Davy, after hearing the news about the Spar-ions on the western border, saddled up and prepared to go assist her siblings, but received word that more Spar-ions were approaching the shores from the northern side. She ran back to the mansion to collect Juliet and all the household servants who could draw sword. Meg Sarah and Juliet mounted a bold attack on the Spar-ions on the northern shore, but they were soon beaten back to the fi-yord.

But while Dick, Joanna, Lucus, and the army fought the Spar-ions on the western border and Meg Sarah and Juliet and the mansion servants engaged the ones in the north, more Spar-ions slipped into Tagawoogah with little or no resistance.

Three days later Davy welcomed a battle-weary Dicken into the Royal Mansion.

"Dicken, what is about foot?" Davy asked anxiously, trying to keep up with his older brother as the latter headed toward the throne-room. Davy was hobbling upon a crutch, his head still bandaged, but his eyes were wide and the lines under them showed he had not slept much since Dick and Joanna had left to pursue the lovis two weeks before.

Dick looked grave. "We come to regroup and get fresh horses, then we ride after stragglers that escaped the battle."

"And Jo and Luke?"

"They are fine," Dick assured his brother. "Seeing to the horses and the troops." He glanced around. "Where are thy sisters?"

"Meg and Juliet only just returned from fighting the Spar-ions on the northern border. They are in their chambers resting."

Dick looked alarmed. "More Spar-ions in the north? Fetch everyone to the throne room for a report."

"It was their plan all along," Dicken said angerly, after hearing Meg

Sarah's report. "Distract us on the one shore whilst the rest of their people slipped around the coast. The chief wasn't even there on the west shore."

Dick sat on his throne surrounded by his five siblings.

"Not just the north," Meg Sarah said. "I have received reports of Spar-ions coming from the east, from the south, from the Borderland. They're everywhere, Dicken. Thousands of Spar-ions have invaded our land and are terrorizing the citizens."

Lucus spoke. "The Iovis have taken the side of Spar-ion."

"Ay," Joanna said thoughtfully. "The Iovis were stirred up and ripe for recruitment by Spar-ion."

Dick stood. "This is war. Spread the word that every creature of Tagawoogah who is able must fight Spar-ion. If'n he is not head of his family, he must join the army. Otherwise, he should protect his own. The Spar-ions must be driven out from our land. If any Iovis is seen aiding our enemies, he must be killed." Dicken looked hard at his siblings. "We have been preparing for such a time as this. Be bold. Be brave. Stay not your hand from either Iovis nor Spar-ion. Show them no mercy. There will be no rest for any Taganian until the last Spar-ion is gone from among us."

Some time later....

Joanna pulled the brush gently through her horse's mane. The morning was quiet for once. Joanna stopped her brushing and leaned against the stallion's neck as she looked around the military encampment. Horses grazed among the hundreds of tents and numerous creatures milled about.

Meg Sarah and some of the troops were back guarding the Royal Mansion. Davy led part of the army against the Spar-ions in the west. Juliet and her troops were pursuing Spar-ion and the Iovis in the Great Wood. And Joanna was here on the plains with Dick and the main army.

"Madame, the king calls for thee."

Joanna turned to see a messenger ready to escort her to Dicken's tent.

Joanna smiled a little and turned back to her horse. "Can't hide out here forever, can I, Storm?" Storm snorted and tossed his head. Joanna slapped the horse's neck and followed the messenger to Dick's tent in the middle of the encampment. She quietly entered. Dick stood with his back toward the entrance.

"You called me?" Joanna asked softly.

"Two years," Dick said. "Two years we have fought Spar-ion. Yet we have not the upper hand." He turned to Joanna. "As of late, it seems that every time we make a move, the Spar-ions already know about it."

"Ay," Joanna agreed. "They seem to know our strategies better than we ourselves."

"It is as if they had an ear in the very chambers of the king," Dick said.

"You suggest there is a traitor among us?" Joanna questioned. "I do not like to think it."

Dick bit his lip. "I do not like to think it either. There is no way we could examine every one in our service."

"What shall we do?" Joanna asked.

Dick sighed. "I know not. Keep your eyes open for any thing amiss."

Joanna nodded.

Dick moved to a map he had spread out on a table, and Joanna followed. "The reports tell us that most of the Spar-ions have gathered here and are moving forward, closer to us," he said, pointing to the place. "But I have heard that a smaller group of Spar-ions, led by the Iovis, are here, just outside the Great Wood."

"Are they a great threat?" Joanna questioned. "The smaller group?"

Dick shook his head. "I think not, but they are too close to the mansion, and I don't like it."

"Meg Sarah has a good defense there," Joanna said. "She can hold off an attack against a small troop if needs be. Beside, the stupid creatures have hemmed themselves in. With Davy on the west, Juliet in the Great Wood, and us here, they cannot move at any how. I say we take on this larger group."

Dick looked thoughtful. "No attempting a surprise attack at night this time," he said. "Not with the traitor in our ranks. Albet we know we cannot fight their main army on the open ground. They outnumber us four to one."

"I say we lead them toward the wood, then," Joanna said in a low voice, pointing to the map. "We already know the Spar-ions cannot fight well in the forest, as they are accustomed to flat ground."

"Split them up," Dick said, nodding as he followed Joanna's train of thought. "Scatter them."

That had been a large part of their strategy in this war. Split the Spar-ions up as much as possible. Thousands of Spar-ions scattered here and there were not as formidable as thousands of Spar-ions together in an army.

"We will advance toward them, then fall back, then advance and fall back, until we have led them into the woods," Dick said. He raked a hand through his longish dark hair. "Someone needs to relieve Juliet and send her to the mansion. Juliet can then send Meg Sarah here. Meg is itching to get back on the field, and we certainly could use a good archer in the wood—no offence, Josey."

"None taken," said Joanna, bowing. Everyone knew that Meg Sarah was the better shot with the bow.

"The messenger must leave without delay," continued Dick.

"I will go," Joanna offered.

"Nigh," Dick said. "I need you to stay and help me rouse the troops. Who is here that we can trust for this mission?"

"Lucus is here. He only just returned last night from a mission in the Borderland," Joanna said.

"Send him in," Dick said, then, "Denatha. I will go to him myself. Prepare the army to move."

Joanna bowed low and took her leave.

A short time later Dick entered Lucus's tent. "Lucus?"

No answer.

The openings in the tent had been covered and Dick could not see anything for a bit while his eyes adjusted to the dim light inside. "Luke?"

Then he spotted his younger brother sitting in a corner with his back to Dick. Lucus's dark hood covered his head.

As Dick moved forward, he saw a flash of light in Lucus's hand.

The Crystal.

"So it was you who brought these wolves to our door," Dick said harshly. "You have brought war to our land."

Lucus did not move or speak.

"Well?" Dick demanded. "What do you have to say for yourself?"

Lucus rose. He slipped the jewel into his pocket. Then he slowly turned to face his brother. Dick's eyes widened when he saw Lucus. Lucus's eyes, usually a lovely blue, were now a gleaming yellow. His face now appeared sunken, his cheekbones prominent. Lucus drew his sword, but instead of advancing toward Dicken, he cut a hole in the tent and slipped out and away.

"We must needs find him," Joanna insisted, when she heard what Dicken told her concerning Lucus. "He must be sick. He needs our help."

"Sick, indeed!" exclaimed Dicken, pacing his tent. "Sick to the head is more like it. 'Tis the accursed token from Spar-ion. It is doing something to him."

"All the more reason we need to find him," Joanna said. "And quickly. Dicken, I will go after him."

"No," Dick said firmly. "I will not let you go until we find out what exactly we are up against. We must needs hear of this Crystal. Send for a prophet."

But none of the prophets of Tagawoogah knew about the symbol, so a Spar-ion priest had to be brought to Dick. The Spar-ion priests were a peaceful folk, and did not fight the Taganians or concern themselves with war. Dicken planned to quietly ship them back to Spar-ion when the war was over.

"'Tis the Crystal of Darkness," the old priest said. "It is the to—"

"I know, I know," Dick said impatiently, with a wave of his hand. "It is the token of your people. Tell me what it does."

"It creates in man a great desire," the priest began again. "Once taken and claimed, it begins to conquer the mind of the one who holds it. It takes over his thoughts. It takes over his feelings. It has plunged Master Lucus into deep darkness."

"In other words, it has turned him against us," Joanna said.

Dick frowned and motioned for the priest to continue.

"The Crystal of Darkness imbeds itself in the victim's's heart. Little by little it works itself in," the priest went on. "Then the person becomes dependent on it. Without the Crystal, he will die. But with the Crystal he will not rest until he kills everyone he cares about."

"Lucus is the spy we have been looking for," Dick said as he resumed his pacing. "I cannot believe I did not see it before. Long our brother hath been working against us."

"How long, pray tell, until the Crystal makes its way into the heart?" Joanna asked the priest.

"Of a surety it has by now," the priest said.

After the priest had been dismissed, Joanna turned to Dick. "Dicken, what must we do?"

Dick had gone back to studying the map. "I fear there is nothing we can do for Lucus," he said gravely. "We can only hope the Crystal has not yet reached his heart, and he is able to resist its power. Remember, whenst I saw him, it was not in his heart."

"So we do nothing?" asked Joanna.

Dick looked up. "He is not hurting us at the present. He did not even turn on me. If anything, we have just rid ourselves of the spy."

"So we just leave him?!" Joanna cried. "He is our brother, Dicken!"

"Joanna, there is nothing we can do for him right now," Dick said firmly. "Lucus wrestles powers we do not understand. The token is dangerous, and now Lucus is dangerous. I will not lose you also. This is his fight, and unless he becomes a direct threat, we do not move on him. That's an order."

"Dicken, this isn't fair," Joanna protested, crossing her arms.

"All's fair in love and war," quoth Dick. "This is both, so 'tis doubly fair, says I."

"Dicken!" protested Joanna. "Listen to yourself, would you?"

"This is final. I will say no more about it," Dick said. "Now go to Meg

Sarah. I will continue the plan."

He turned back to his map. Joanna bit her lip. Anyone could see that she did not agree with her brother's decision. But she bowed and took her leave.

As she entered the horse enclosure, a samanta offered to prepare her horse. But Joanna shook her head and waved him away. Storm was her special horse and she did not let anyone else touch him. She'd saddle him herself.

Joanna found some peace in talking over the situation concerning Lucus with her sister Meg Sarah. As they sat together in the mansion's garden, Meg Sarah explained why she agreed with Dick on the matter. "It is good that we wait and see how it plays out. I mean, we don't know that Lucus is bad. Just like Dicken said."

"It makes no sense to me. If'n the Spar-ions only came here for the Crystal, and Lucus has the Crystal, and Lucus is with the Spar-ions, then the Spar-ions have the Crystal. Why do they not leave, then?" Joanna wondered aloud.

Meg Sarah shrugged. "Then maybe Lucus is not with the Spar-ions."

"Or mayhap the Spar-ions used the Crystal as a distraction," Joanna said. "A means to start a war. Of a surety they mean to kill us and take our land, and the Crystal was but an excuse. Ach, my sister! The matter maketh me restless."

"I am restless living here in luxury whilst everyone else is on the field," Meg Sarah said. "My arm was good as new weeks ago. I don't know why Dicken pulled me off the field. He freaks out too much." Meg Sarah had

had her arm injured during a fight with the Iovis in the Hill Country, and Dick had insisted she rest for a while back at the Royal Mansion.

"I will go then," Joanna said, smiling. "I will send Juliet to take over for you, and you may join Dicken."

It had been hardly a fortnight since Joanna had taken over leadership of Juliet's troop in the Great Wood. Joanna was sitting outside her tent sharpening her sword when two of her soldiers came to her, bringing with them a third.

"Lady Joannas, here is one that has somewhat to tell thee."

Joanna looked up and recognized the third as one of the captains of Dicken's army.

"Ah. What news have ye from the king?" she asked. "Prithee speak."

The creature, a Samoi, folded his hands and glanced at the soldiers around him nervously.

"A private matter, Madame. I wish an audience with only you," said he, bowing.

"Very well," Joanna said, nodding to the others to take their leave.

"Now, pray tell," Joanna said, once the two were settled. "Is it a personal message from Richard?"

"Nay," replied the creature. "He wist not that I am here."

"Ay?" said Joanna curiously.

"My brother, Urak, has been accused of aiding the Iovis. I fear he will be sentenced to death. I beg you to come speak on his behalf. You are my only hope, Madame. I know the king will listen to you."

"I will go back with you," Joanna said.

"It wasn't him," protested Joanna. "Urak would never betray your trust."

Joanna and Richard were in the council tent, arguing. Or rather, Joanna was arguing.

"You heard the troops speak out against him," Dick said. "The word is strong."

"Nay, but it meaneth anon," cried Joanna. "It is a time of war, Dicken. The troops are tired. Afraid. They will say what they will. Their testimony cannot be counted at a time like this. You of all people should know that. Beside, they said what they thought you wanted to hear. You had already decided that Urak was guilty even before the trial started."

"This discussion is over, Joanna. My word stands. Urak is to be executed in the morning."

"It is most certainly not over, Dicken," said Joanna, her temper flaring. "Do you not know who Urak is? His family has been loyal servants to us for many years. His ancestors served Shelton himself in the Royal Mansion."

"I know all this," said Dick. "Albet you do not know how hard this is for me. You come flying back here to point your finger of judgement at me at a time when my friends have become my enemies."

"I came back to save a life," said Joanna, indignant. "I came back to save you from killing a faithful servant."

"I say again, Joannas," Dick said sternly, "My word stands. Nothing you say or do will convince me that the creature is not guilty."

That night Urak escaped from the holding cells and left the camp.

"He was aided, my king," said the guard who was giving Richard the report the next morning. "We have combed the camp, albet Urak is no where to be found. Shall we search the surrounding regions?"

"No," replied Dicken. "He is a cunning creature, and I am sure he is long gone by now."

There was a small sound near the entrance to the tent, and Dicken looked up to see Joanna standing there. He waved the guard away, and Joanna approached him. She bowed.

"Permission to return to my troop, my liege," she murmered, her eyes on the floor.

"Permission granted."

Joanna straighted and turned to leave.

"Urak escaped last night," Dick said, and Joanna stopped, her back to Richard.

"So I have heard," said Joanna quietly.

"I will find out who is responsible for this. I hope for your sake that I do not discover that you were involved, Joannas."

Joanna made no answer, just bowed her head slightly and left the tent.

* In Tagawoogah, it was proper that you ask permission of the general before leaving a military fort or establishment of any kind. The reason

being, of course, that you might be needed. If any one entered a military establishment, he or she involuntary put himself and everyone with him, under the commanding officer, for the duration of their stay.

A Few Months Later...

"The forts on the river are lost." The speaker was Juliet, dirty and battle weary, but still standing tall before her king. "We exhausted our efforts, but there wasn't much we could do. The banks were overrun even before we got there."

Dick sighed and rubbed his forehead with his fingers.

Juliet watched him. "I'm sorry, Dicken."

"No, Juliet, it is I who should be sorry. You did all you could. I did not send you with enough troops or resources to secure the forts. I underestimated the situation."

"You didn't know, Dicken."

"But I should have."

"No, Dicken."

There was a moment of silence, then Juliet spoke. "If you send me with more troops, I will march out in the morning to re-take the forts."

"No," said Dicken. "Leave the forts. It will take more effort to re-capture them than they are worth. We have more important things to attend to. Our possession of Zur-thon is essential to my battle strategy in the West. The strongholds at Zur cannot be lost. Fetch Meg Sarah."

Juliet bowed and left.

A few moments later, Meg Sarah entered his tent and bowed before her brother. "You sent for me?"

"Ay," answered Dick. "The citizens of Zur-thon need assistance in driving the Iovis from their land. I am sending you to their aid."

Meg Sarah was quiet, staring down at the ground.

"Is there a problem?" Dick asked impatiently.

Meg Sarah looked up at him. "I have heard rumors that Lucus is with the Iovis at Zur-thon," she said quietly.

Dick shrugged. "It may not be true."

"But it also may be," Meg Sarah said. "I will not go. I cannot kill a brother."

Dick raised an eyebrow. "You defy an order from your king?"

Meg Sarah lowered her eyes. "I meant no disrespect."

Joanna, who was standing nearby, came to her sister's aid. "Send me, pray," she said, stepping forward.

Dick looked hard at Joanna. "You know that Lucus is no longer the brother you remember. You know he has changed, consumed by the Crystal of Darkness. You know this, and how he seeks to kill us."

"Ay," Joanna murmured. "I will do what must be done."

Dick looked at her for a long moment. Joanna squirmed under his intense gaze. Did Dicken know about her plan? Finally he nodded. "Go.

Take Juliet with you. May the Mark of the Master be good upon thee."

"What's the hurry?" Juliet asked as she urged her horse to keep up with Joanna on Storm. "Have you not killed enough Iovis to satisfy you already?"

Joanna did not slow down. "We have to find Lucus before some one else does."

"Joanna—" Juliet started to protest.

"Trust me, Juliet. Just trust me on this."

After many days of searching, the two girls found Lucus in a thicket. Peering through the bushes, Joanna and Juliet studied the boy, who was kneeling on the ground, rocking back and forth.

Lucus let out a groan. The Crystal was in his head, in his heart, everywhere. It was taking over, driving Lucus insane. He must get it out. Yes, that was what to do. Pulling his Sword from its sheath, he studied the blade. Surely it was better to die than to live as a servant to the Crystal, he decided.

When Juliet saw what Lucus was preparing to do, she moved to stop him, but Joanna held her back. "Stay," she said.

"What?" Juliet hissed. "He's going to kill himself! I cannot stay!"

"Nigh, Juliet. Watch," Joanna whispered.

Lucus seemed to hesitate then, as if having second thoughts. "Come on, Lucus," Joanna begged silently from her hiding place. With a strangled cry, Lucus fell upon his sword and drove the blade of it deep into his heart.

"No!" cried Juliet, struggling against Joanna's hold.

Lucus lay on the ground, gasping for air, blood flowing swiftly from beneath the sword. With his remaining strength, Lucus twisted and turned the blade, finally digging the Crystal of Darkness from his heart. Then he closed his eyes and sighed as he leaned down upon his sword.

"Lucus!" Juliet shrieked, tears streaming down her cheeks. Joanna let Juliet go, and the younger girl rushed to Lucus, pushing him onto his back. "No, Lucus, no, Lucus. Stay with me!" Juliet sobbed, lowering her face to his. "You can't die, Lucus. Lucus! Lucus, don't leave us."

Joanna came running with canteens and began to pour water over Lucus. She pulled the sword from his chest and destroyed the Crystal on the blood-soaked ground.

"What are you doing?!" Juliet looked up from Lucus just long enough to holler at her older sister. Wasn't this whole thing Joanna's fault in the first place?

"It's okay, Juliet," Joanna said calmly, putting Lucus's sword down gently by his side.

"Okay?!" yelled Juliet. "How can any of this be o—"

She stopped and stared in wonder as the flesh of Lucus's chest began to miraculously move to cover the wound.

"The water from the Healing Pool," she whispered, her eyes wide. "Joanna, how did you—"

Joanna just smiled and put her arm around Juliet. The two sisters sat and watched until Lucus's wound was just a small scar over his heart.

"Now be sure to tell Dicken that Lucus cut the stone from him himself," Joanna instructed Juliet as she led her sister's horse through the forest. They had found a pack horse to come behind and carry Lucus, who was still unconscious. "Tell Meg Sarah that Lucus is fine and not to worry herself over him. Assure her he will recover in a few days."

"I will, Joanna," said Juliet. She looked her older sister over in wonder. "You must have been planning this, Jo. You got the water from the pool at just the right time so it was still potent when we found Lucus. You knew he would attempt to take his life, did you not?"

Joanna only smiled and did not answer. The trio came to a stop on a little rise. "Here, Juliet. I have led you to the right path. You know your way from here." She patted the horse's neck and stepped back. "Off you go, little one."

But Juliet held her horse still. "You did not answer my question, Jo."

Joanna smiled and reached up to pat her sister's hand. "Nay, I thought I would have to cut the Crystal from Lucus's heart myself. I was glad I did not have to. Now go on, Juliet. The daylight is being wasted."

"Where are you going, Joanna?" Juliet asked.

Joanna had turned and was mounting Storm, who had followed a small distance behind the pack horse. She flashed a grin. "Well, someone has to help the Zur-thons drive the lovis out."

Lucus splashed cold water on his face from the basin and dabbed his skin dry with the inside of his cloak. It had been several months since he had cut the Crystal of Darkness from his heart, and it was certainly good to finally be back to his usual self. Now he had to gain Dick's trust back. That had been a slow process. At least now Dicken allowed Lucus on the field, even though he had Juliet and Meg Sarah watching him.

"The king commeth! Make way for the king!" The troops took up the lookout's call one by one until the news seemed to echo through the camp.

Lucus adjusted his hanbirk and strode to where Meg Sarah and Juliet stood ready to meet Dicken.

As Dick alighted from his horse, the three bowed and murmured their greetings. Dicken's gaze traveled quickly over the girls, then seemed to linger on Lucus. "Do you have a large tent?" he asked Meg Sarah, still looking at Lucus.

"Ay, right this way. Come in and we will talk," Meg Sarah said.

Once the four were alone, Juliet inquired after Joanna and Davy.

"Both well," Dicken reported. "Joanna returned not long ago from the Zur-thon and is at the Royal Mansion as we speak. Davy marches this way after leading a successful campaign against the lovis in the Hill Country."

Dick looked around at the trio. "There hath been fighting here?" he inquired.

"No," Lucus said sarcastically. "We've been just sitting about and playing fiddlesticks whilest Juliet draws us pictures of the lovis dying terrible deaths."

"What Lucus is meaning to say," Juliet said, frowning at her second brother, "Is that this has been a hard front. We have had hard fighting and many losses. We have only just now begun to drive the Iovis and the Spar-ions back to the wood."

Meg Sarah nodded, agreeing with Juliet.

Dick looked thoughtful. "I have received word that the chief of Spar-ion leadeth an army toward the Valley of Salt. He means to meet us in battle at the rising of the blood-moon."

"Then we must needs meet him," Meg Sarah said. "We have been looking for the chief for all these years."

"Now he shows himself?" Juliet mused thoughtfully. "What meaneth it? I sense a trap."

"Trap or no, we must get to the chief and end this war," Dicken said. "If'n he cannot be convinced to lead his countrymen back to Spar-ion, we kill him. Once their chief is dead, the Spar-ions will fall easily, as will the Iovis. We bring all our forces together and march on the morrow. One of us will stay with a small troop to guard the Mansion. The rest of us will go."

"Who will stay in the Mansion?' asked Lucus. He knew full well that none of his siblings would want to stay and miss the greatest and, if Dick was right, final, big battle of the war.

"I have thought of that," Dick said. "Whomever's star doth not appear to-night, those will stay." The others nodded.

"Fair enough," Lucus said.

Juliet stepped from her tent, pulling her cloak about her tightly to shield her body from the chilly night air. She spotted Dick on his back in the grass a short distance away, both his lions at his feet. Juliet went over and joined her oldest brother, and the two gazed silently up into the clear night sky.

"I wish I never had to do it," said Dicken suddenly.

"Do what, Dicken?" questioned Juliet.

"Every day I send my younger brothers and sisters into harm's way," Dick said.

Juliet turned and studied him. "It must be a heavy burden."

"It is indeed. One that will very soon fall from me."

There was silence as Juliet contemplated Dicken's words, then she spoke. "Dick, you don't have to do this, you know. March out to meet the chieftain. He teases you. Like a snake he crawls from his hole to taunt you. I know he is up to no good."

"Ay," returned the boy, thoughtfully, "but though I know not what I will face to-morrow, I am ready to face it, be it for good or for ill. There is no peace without war, Juliet. No victory without struggle. The lives of mortals are like grass; they flourish like a flower of the field, but the battle of good and evil has been raging since the beginning of time."

"Is there no hope, then, Dicken?" Juliet questioned.

"Nay, on the contrary, sister," replied Dick. "There is always hope. Where there is yet life, there is yet hope."

The two fell silent again for a space.

"The star of Jetta hideth itself to-night," Juliet observed.

"Ay," said Dicken. "Meg Sarah will stay."

Juliet studied her eldest brother. "You take on too much of a burden, Dicken. You feel that everything that happens is your fault. That everything is your responsibility. Believe me, Dicken, once you start down that path, there's no going back."

"I am already down that path, Juliet. I condemned a loyal servant of the Royal Mansion to death, and he was killed by the Iovis while trying to escape me. He was innocent, Juliet. He did nothing. I was blind. And if I had not approved of the journey over the Saka, we would not be at war right now."

"Dick, you can't blame yourself. You didn't know."

Juliet rolled onto her side so she could face Dick. "Whatever you are to face to-morrow, we are ready to face with you, Dicken. All of us."

Dick smiled a tight smile. "Thank you, Juliet. I will remember that."

Juliet studied him. "Promise?"

"Promise," Dick said, and Juliet snuggled up against him.

By midday on the third day they had almost reached the Valley of Salt. Dick led the way, Lucus beside him. Juliet and Joanna rode on each flank of the great company, and Davy brought up the rear.

"Now remember, Lucus," Dick instructed, "You and Joanna are leading the troops. I will disguise myself and pursue the chief. You are not to stray from your mission, no matter what."

"Ay, Master," said Lucus. Dick's repetition of the battle plan was hardly necessary. Lucus had just regained Dicken's trust and was determined to do all that was required of him so as not to break it again.

The troop halted when they were almost within sight of the valley so Joanna could ride up and take her place beside Lucus, and Dicken could slip away to change clothes and otherwise disguise himself. Joanna patted Storm's neck and glanced sideways at her younger brother. "You ready for this?"

Lucus looked grim. "I only hope the chief is there after all this." He tightened his grip on his horse's reins and took a deep breath. "Let's do this thing."

Joanna nodded and turned in her saddle. "Company, forward!"

Dick dodged two struggling creatures and ran a third through with his ax as he plunged on. Finding a chief in the chaos of a battle was certainly not easy. It did not help matters that Dick was on foot. But the chief must not find out who he was, and his disguise called for the king of Tagawoogah to leave his horse behind. Suddenly he stopped. There! Was that the chief? Dick ducked down and strained his eyes to get a closer look through the mass of moving bodies. But while Dick so hesitated, he was dealt a heavy blow from behind. Dick felt the breath whoosh from him as he fell flat on his face to the ground. He made himself get up to avoid being trampled underfoot and scolded himself for not paying better attention to the battle. There was a rocky crag on the outskirts of the valley, and to this Dick stumbled. Propping himself up on a rock, he ran his fingers carefully over the wound in his back to access the damages. The area seemed to be mostly just badly bruised. Not life-threatening. Now to catch his breath... But, alas, the chief of the Spar-ions himself stood over Dick, spear in his hand.

"Richard," he growled.

So much for the disguise, Dick thought.

"Chieftain," Dicken said, "Halt your troops."

The chief threw his head back and laughed. "That not will I," he said lustily.

"The Crystal has been destroyed," Dick said. "Why do you not return to your home world and leave us in peace?"

The chief laughed again. "Crystal? What do you take me for, Richard? I care not for the Crystal. I want your sister for my son, and I want your land. I want your throne. I want your power. And now," he added, moving toward Dick, "I will have your blood." Dick looked for a route of escape, but four husky Spar-ion warriors had surrounded him whilst he was talking to the chief. The chief's bodyguards. This did not look good. Dick had lost his ax when he fell, leaving him weaponless. But Joanna came to Dick's aid. Jumping down from a rocky outcropping above them, she landed squarely on her feet between Dick and the chief.

"Touch him, and I'll rip your throat out, you mangy cur," she declared, sword aloft and eyes blazing.

"Ah. Those be fighting words, Joannas," said the chief.

"Ay. And you have picked a fight with the wrong person," Joanna said. The four Spar-ion warriors moved to assist their leader, but Joanna slipped Dick his sword behind her back and, leaving him to dispatch the chief's bodyguards, she took on the chief herself.

The noise of battle grew quiet and the sun began to slip down over the horizon. Dick, Juliet, and Lucus had gone, pursuing the Spar-ions who had fled the battle. But still Joanna fought the chief. The girl was growing weary, but some inner spark kept her going. That, and the instinct to survive. Then Davy ended the business and speared the chief from behind so that he fell dead at Joanna's feet.

"I was getting kind of sick of the guy," he said.

But when the Six regrouped and returned the next day to the Royal Mansion, they found only a pile of smoking ruins. A troop of Iovis and Spar-ions had burned the Mansion and taken Meg Sarah captive.

"We must mount a rescue and get Meg Sarah back," declared Lucus.

Dick was sitting on a chair, stripped to the waist, while Juliet tended his wounds. "No, Lucus," he said tiredly. "Not right now. We wait for the right moment. Meg Sarah will not be harmed."

"But Dicken—" he protested.

"Enough, Lucus," said Juliet, scowling at him. "You heard Dicken. The matter is closed."

"No, it is not closed," Lucus snapped, temper flaring. "This is between me and Dicken. Back out, Juliet."

"Take a walk, Lucus," said Davy.

Dick held up his hand. "I don't like this any more than you do, Lucus. When the time is right, I will send you to retrieve Meg Sarah. For now, you must be patient. There is much to be done. Without their chief, the Spar-ions are scattered. We cannot let them regroup."

Lucus bit his lip and crossed his arms. Which was worse-- having his sister in the filthy hands of their enemies or having Dick stop trusting him again?

Lucus followed Joanna from the tent. "Jo, you have to speak to Dicken. We can't just forget about Meg Sarah."

Joanna sighed. "You heard Dicken. His mind is made up."

"Joanna—" Lucus began. Joanna turned and interrupted him.

"Lucus, look. I know it's hard, but we have to trust Dicken's judgement. We have to trust that we will have a better opportunity to get Meg Sarah back. Sir Richard has never steered us wrong before, has he?"

"No," Lucus agreed grudgingly. "But even a king is wrong sometimes." He studied Joanna. "You know something."

"Okay." Joanna looked around carefully and lowered her voice. "Remember whenst the Spar-ions cared for Meg Sarah when she was sick?"

Lucus shrugged. "Yeah, so?"

"Dick told me that when he heard the chieftain speaking to his son in the courtyard, the chieftain said to kill the men from across the Saka. They never intended to kill Meg Sarah. To get her was one of the goals of the chieftain. He wants her alive. And Dick must be very sure of this, so we trust his judgement."

Two weeks later, Dick called Lucus before him. "It is time," he said. "Go get Meg Sarah. I have received word the Iovis have left her in the care of the Samoi of the mountains whilst they march to the Deviding

Range."

Lucus bowed and prepared to take his leave, but Dick stopped him.

"Lucus," he said, "remember that the Samoi are a peaceful folk. They have no say in this war. They keep Meg Sarah only because the Iovis would have hurt them if they did not. They wilt most willingly give Meg Sarah over to thee. Remember this, and deal with the Samoi accordingly."

"Ay, master," Lucus said, leaving the room.

But when Lucus came to the Samoi village and saw Meg Sarah tied up in the midst of it, his anger came upon him hotly and he slew with his sword every male, female, and little one in his path. Once he freed Meg Sarah from her bonds, she also drew sword, and together Lucus and Meg Sarah slaughtered the Samoi in the village until there was none left.

But no sooner had they finished this then they heard the sound of an army approaching.

"'Tis the Spar-ion," said Meg Sarah. "They have come for me. Hurry, Lucus. We must flee. There are too many of them."

Lucus was not one to run from a fight, but when he saw the army, he quickly agreed with his sister. The two took to their heels. As they ran, however, Meg Sarah fell into a trap, spraining her ankle. Lucus ran a few paces, but when he realized his sister was no longer beside him, he went back to her.

"Go on!" Meg Sarah urged him. "Hurry! Go, Lucus! Don't worry about me!"

"I will not leave you," Lucus said stubbornly, as he began to cut the cords of the trap to free his sister.

Meg Sarah looked behind them and saw that the army was approaching. "Lucus, they've seen us! Just go, Lucus!" she begged. "The Spar-ions won't hurt me. The son of the chieftain likes me. But they will kill you. Now go!"

"I won't leave you," Lucus repeated.

"Would you leave if you were assured of my safety?" Meg Sarah asked, still looking back at the army.

"Not I," Lucus said. "Even if I were guaranteed of your safety, how could I look thy brother in the face if I return without thee?"

And with that, Lucus heaved Meg Sarah onto his back and kept running.

Meanwhile, Joanna and Dick waited for Lucus at the Royal Mansion.

"Alack! What aileth the chap that he tarry so?" Dick wondered aloud. "Lucus could have returned twice from the mountains by now."

"Mayhap he got into some trouble," Joanna said.

"I sent him into neutral territory to fetch his sister from some peaceful Samoi. It would take some blundering fool to botch that mission," Dick said.

Joanna shrugged. "Who knows? Our Lucus is a talented one."

Dick grunted. "Well, send him in as soon as he gets here. We have wasted enough time already."

It was nearly mid-afternoon when Lucus made his way slowly into the compound, Meg Sarah unconscious on his back. Household servants hurried to relieve Lucus of his burden. "Is Meg okay?" Joanna asked anxiously as she came from the courtyard.

"She's fine," Lucus said. "Sprained ankle."

"And it looks like she hasn't eaten or slept in days," Joanna said, examining her sister. "Bring her to her chamber," she instructed the servants.

Lucus sighed and rubbed his sore shoulders and back against a post. "Now for a good meal and a hot bath," he said.

"I think not. You are to report to Dicken right away," quoth Joanna.

Lucus frowned. "Now?"

"Ay, he said as soon as you get back," Joanna replied. Lucus grunted and headed in the direction of the court, and Joanna went back to what she was doing.

While walking past Juliet's chamber, she noticed movement behind the curtain. She paused. "Sister?"

"Come in, Jo," Juliet said from within.

Joanna entered, and saw that Juliet was packing her bags.

"You're leaving? So soon?"

"Ay. I and my company ride post-haste for Kettley at first morning light. The lovis disagreement," said Juliet, adding a jacket to a bundle.

"Ah," said Joanna. "You got that fun job." She sat down at the edge of her sister's cot. "If it were up to me, I'd say we let the lovis fight and kill each other off. I think it is a waste of time and resources to get involved at this point."

Juliet smiled. "My sentiments exactly. But I'm just following orders. Dick always has a method in his madness after all. Maybe he thinks a show of force will sway the remaining Iovis to our side."

Joanna snorted. "Not likely. Probably just make them angry."

"I know it. If that is the case, Dicken better not hold his breath."

"Lucus," Dick ordered as soon as he spotted his younger brother. "Run to our camp on the eastern border and bring Davy this message." He handed him a roll of parchment.

"Run?" Lucus panted. "By my sooth, I can barely stand."

"Have one of the horses saddled, then," Dicken said impatiently. "Go now."

Lucus bowed and took his leave.

Shortly thereafter Joanna came in to see Dick. She was upset.

"Dick, do you know what Lucus has done?"

"Lucus?" Dick said. "Alack, the selfsame was here not ten minutes anon." He studied Joanna's flushed face. "Pray tell, what has he done?"

"He killed them, Dicken! He killed the whole Samoi village. Just wiped out a peaceful tribe. They are gone! All gone, Dicken!"

Dick slammed his fist down on the table as he stood. "Stupid boy! As if I didn't have enough problems with the Spar-ion and the Iovis, he has to go start a war with the Samoi!"

The next day a messenger came to the Royal Mansion.

"'Tis a Samoi priest from the Ridge," Joanna informed Dick. "He is a representative of the chief."

Dick groaned. "Great. Where is our diplomatic relations manager when we need her?"

"Juliet is leading a company to Kettley."

"I was not requesting an answer," Dick muttered.

"Juliet could not help us at any how," said Joanna. "The priest refuses to speak to anyone but the king himself."

"Oh, wonderful," Dick said sarcastically. "I'm flattered."

"This is serious, Dick. You need to convince the Samoi representative that we had not a hand in the slaughter of his people," Joanna began. "Lucus was acting of his own free will. You must needs convince him. We cannot afford a war with the Samoi. They may appear peaceful, but when any of their people are threatened, they fight like mad."

"I know all this," Dick growled. "Send him in."

Joanna did not move. "You are angry, Dicken."

"Ay, angry at Lucus, that I am."

"You need to calm yourself before addressing the representative."

"I am calm," Dick snapped.

Joanna lifted her chin. "You should listen to me sometimes, you know, Dicken. I am your advisor."

"And I am your king," returned Dicken, tone icy as he glared at Joanna. "You would do well to remember your place."

Joanna turned and left the room, mumbling something about Dick doing something he would later regret.

The Samoi priest came and bowed before Dick. "My master saith, 'Why hast thou raised a hand against the unarmed?'"

"Far be it from me!" Dick returned. "I do not harm innocents."

"What say you then of the mountain village?" the priest inquired. "No male, female, or child survived."

"Ah! That would be Barak-San," Dick said. "And I assure you, I knew nothing of this. I would never grant approval for such a thing. Lucus acted of his own accord, and that foolishly."

The priest studied Dick. "Then you did not give the order to desolate our village?"

"I did not."

"Will you swear by the Great One that you had no hand in the slaughter of the innocent, as afore mentioned?"

"I will swear it."

As was the custom in Tagawoogah, Dick placed a hand over his heart and repeated the oath after the priest to swear it.

"I had no part in the murder of the Samoi in the mountain. I had no knowledge of the attack nor did I plan it. My hands are clean of innocent blood."

But instead of stopping after Dick repeated the required oath, the

Samoi priest went on.

"Cursed be Barak-San among all his brethren! As lighting strikes a tree, so let wrath strike that youth. May disaster come upon him swiftly so that he cannot escape it. Let the days of San-Barak be few and evil, and may his seed die with him."

Finished, the Samoi priest left the room.

At a nod from Dicken, Joanna followed the priest to see him out. But when Joanna found him, he was standing outside the chamber where Meg Sarah lay. His hand on the curtain, the priest was muttering something.

Coming closer, Joanna made out some of his words. "...and though she marry the one she loveth and bear him sons, may she never find joy in him...."

Joanna spoke up. "Is it not enough that you curse my brother that you curse my sister also?"

The old priest slowly turned to face her. "Joannas, your mind deceiveth thee. Know ye not that your sister also had a hand in the slaughter of the innocent? But now that you have spoken against the curse, you also shall have a part in the evil to come."

The priest made his way out of the mansion, and Joanna returned to the throne room.

"Well, that went well," said Dicken.

"So saith the man who cursed his own brother," said Joanna, crossing her arms.

"I spoke not a word against the selfsame," Dick argued.

"Nay," quoth Joanna, "But you had a hand over your heart whilst the priest cursed Lucus, so you were affirming the oath."

"Mayhap Lucus deserves to be cursed, Joanna, have you ever thought of that?" Dick said, raising his voice a little.

"No one deserves to be cursed," Joanna said quietly.

About a year after the death of the Spar-ion chief, the majority of the Spar-ions had been driven back to the sea and taken their ships back toward their land. Now that the Spar-ions were no longer a major threat, the Noble Six turned their attention to the Iovis, who had only been a small part of the war before. But the Iovis had strengthened themselves during the time the Noble Six made war with Spar-ion. The support of Spar-ion had made them bold, and the shifted focus had enabled them to take many strategic military positions around Tagawoogah.

Meg Sarah and Lucus were stationed in the Woodland when they heard news that Davy's force, who had been engaging the enemy on the Western Banks, had been overrun; and Davy had been taken captive to the Old Fortress, which was then controlled by the Iovis. Lucus was of mind to take some of the troops and to march on the fortress and get Davy back, but Meg Sarah said, "Wait, brother. Joanna and Dicken are to be here on the morrow. We will talk with them about what is to be done. They will mount a mission to rescue Davy. And if'n they decide to move on the fortress, we will then have two armies instead of one."

But during the night Lucus took some of the troops and stole away.

When Joanna and Dicken rode into the camp at sunrise, Meg Sarah ran to tell them what happened. "Lucus slipped away during the night. I did not know that he left. He was of mind to lay siege to the Old Fortress where Davy is imprisoned. He is probably there already."

"Whyk!?" exclaimed Dicken. "Even if he had an army twice this size, he would not stand a chance against the fortress."

"He took fewer than a hundred with him," Meg Sarah said, worried. "I tried to tell him—"

Dick growled in disgust. "Is he not Barak-San? And doth not the curse of Barak-San follow him? What shall be done with him?"

"When they feel threatened, the Iovis kill their captives," Joanna said, looking at Dick. "If Lucus attacks the fortress, Davy may be killed."

"Ay, and Lucus also," Dick said grimly. "Come, Joanna. We must ride hard. Meg Sarah, you will stay with the troops and wait for word."

"Ay, master," Meg Sarah said. She bowed her head and whispered a prayer for her younger brothers as she watched Dick and Joanna gallop away.

Joanna and Dicken pulled their mounts to a halt on a distant hill overlooking the fortress. Lucus and his company had almost reached the stronghold. The troop was as a small black dot in the Old Fortress's shadow. Joanna imagined the Iovis laughing behind their strong walls at the tiny army that dared come against them.

"The boy is daft!" she exclaimed.

Dick set his mouth in a firm line. "You get Davy, and I'll get Lucus."

Joanna turned to go, but Dick stopped her. "Joanna, do not engage. I repeat, do not engage. Get Davy and get out of there as fast as you can."

"Ay, master."

Joanna and Dick parted ways as they headed toward the fortress.

Joanna paused under a lone tree to pull the hood of her cloak over her head. The sprinkle of rain had turned into a steady drizzle. Thunder rumbled in the distance. Kneeling, Joanna dug some mud from the ground and used it to cover her face. She had brought some red earthen paint, and she used this to paint her face after the fashion of the Iovis. The sky was quickly becoming darker, though it was early afternoon. Wetting a finger, she held it up to check the wind speed and direction. Everything was perfect. Now was the time.

As she had expected, Joanna easily entered the fortress and slipped down to the dungeons without detection. The storm and the attack on the wall had the Iovis sufficiently distracted.

A lone guard stood in front of Davy's cell. Joanna spoke to him in Iovis, and he handed her a set of keys and left. Joanna unlocked the cell and went to her little brother. "Davy."

"Joanna? Is it you?" the boy rasped.

"Ay. I'm getting you out of here. Can you walk?"

"I can."

"Then let us be gone from this foul place."

Meanwhile Dick was in the valley trying to find Lucus. The darkening sky and the driving rain combined with the noise and chaos of the battle made the task increasingly difficult. I can't believe I'm doing this, Dick thought as he urged his horse Lladimir through the fray. Lucus's troops, who had once been in ordered ranks, now were scattered everywhere, fighting enemies one-on-one. This is mayhem. Where is Lucus?

Finally he spotted him. "Lucus!" he hollered as he came near. No response. Lucus could not hear him. Dick drew closer. "Lucus! Lucus, this is madness! Call your troops back!"

"No!" Lucus shouted.

"Lucus, you cannot win this! Tell your troops to fall back!" Dick yelled again.

Lucus did not reply, only spurred his mount onward to get away from his older brother. Dick growled in frustration and pursued Lucus. When Lladimir was side-by-side with Lucus's horse, Dick leaped from his saddle and tackled Lucus. The boys landed on the muddy ground with a thud, Dick on top of Lucus. Lucus was the first to catch his breath. He struggled out from under Dick and turned to escape, but Dick knocked him on the back of the head with a nearby axe handle. He heaved the unconscious Lucus onto Lladimir's back with the help of a nearby soldier and mounted behind him. Then Dick blew the trumpet and rode through the ranks, yelling, "Retreat! Retreat! Fall back! Back to the camp! To camp! Retreat! Rally behind your king!"

Joanna sat by the fire in her tent back at camp, watching as Davy ate some warm soup.

The tent flap parted, and Joanna looked up as Meg Sarah entered and went to the fire to warm her hands. "How is Lucus?" Joanna asked her sister.

"A bump on the head," Meg Sarah said. "He'll be fine. It's Dicken I'm worried about."

"Dick?" questioned Joanna. "What is wrong with—"

"Lucus's shinanagins must not go unpunished this time," came an angry voice from outside the tent.

"See?" mouthed Meg Sarah as Dick entered.

"This latest escapade trumps them all. Lucus must be punished," Dick raved, pacing the tent.

"Lucus was only trying to save Davy—" Meg Sarah began, but Dick cut her off.

"Was only?!" cried he. "Was only?! This is now the third time Lucus has defied me. He made a military move without the approval of his king, and deliberately disobeyed a direct order on the field. Because of him, most of my best troops are dead. And his foolhardiness could have cost Davy his life."

Joanna, Meg Sarah, and Davy all looked at each other. Dicken had a point. Lucus did indeed need to be punished. If Lucus got away with pulling a stunt like that, then all of their troops would do as they pleased. All of Tagawoogah would see the Six as weak and not fit to rule if Lucus went unpunished.

"It is high time we make an publick example of Lucus," Dick continued. "Every one must see what happens when the king's order is counted anon." He looked at Davy and his two sisters. There was silence.

"Well?" Dick asked his advisors impatiently.

"The traitor's price is twenty lashes," Joanna offered.

Meg Sarah gave her a you're-not-helping look, then turned to Dick to plead on Lucus's behalf. "Pray, Dicken, this is madness. Surely we must keep our heads in this. There must be another punishment more fit. Lucus does not deserve to be so scorned."

"Doesn't he?" Dicken demanded. "You always stick up for him, don't you?"

"I stick up for all my brothers," Meg Sarah said quietly. "That is what makes us family."

"Well, here 'tis no room for family in this matter," Dick said firmly. "This is for him also. For all of us. My word is final. Lucus is to receive the lashes."

The next morning Lucus was called before the king to hear his sentence, as befit his station.

Lucus bowed before Dick and then stood at attention.

"You do know that you have done wrong," Dick said, scrutinizing his younger brother.

Lucus lowered his eyes. "Ay," he murmured, with all the repentance he could manage.

"And I suppose you also know that you deserve to be punished," Dick continued.

"Ay."

When Dick read his sentence, Lucus did not flinch.

"Do you have anything to say for yourself?" Dick asked after.

Lucus bowed again. "I have committed treason. Do what seemeth good to you. Only one thing do I ask, and one only."

Dick nodded. "Speak, for I will not refuse you."

"Let, prithee, thy servant receive twenty-five lashes. Let it never be said that Vonna-Sias is a traitor. His heart is with the king withal."

"It is done."

When Lucus turned away, Joanna looked at Dicken and saw tears in his eyes. Regardless of Dick's strong exterior on the matter, punishing his own brother was tough for him. Even though he did what he must, Dick still loved Lucus. And Joanna regarded both her brothers very brave in the matter.

So Lucus was tied in the midst of the camp and flogged before Dick and all the officers and soldiers. Davy, Joanna, and Meg Sarah stood with Dicken, their faces grave. Meg Sarah had said that she would not watch Lucus's humiliation, but Dick had insisted that it was important they were all there. It showed that they agreed with Dick's sentence and they were all one in the matter.

Lucus stayed in a tent without the camp for seven days. During this time, Meg Sarah tended to his wounds. At the end of the days appointed him, Lucus asked for an audience with the king.

Joanna held her breath as Lucus came and bowed before his king, face to the ground. What would Dicken do? Lucus had been punished and was repentant. Would Dick now accept him back as if nothing had happened?

There was a long pause, then Dick's face broke into a smile and he went to pull Lucus to his feet and hug him.

It was several months later when Davy, who had been fighting with Lucus on the western front, rode into the camp of Meg Sarah and Joanna. He had ridden hard for many miles, but there was no time to rest until he had completed his mission. He slid from his saddle and hurried to find his sisters. "Lucus is badly wounded," he said, breathless. "The doctors can do nothing for him. They say he will be dead by the morrow."

"I will go to him," Meg Sarah said, without hesitation. "Davy, saddle my horse. I will get my things. We must make haste."

Joanna stood still for a moment, then hurried after Davy, who had gone to get the horse. "Nay, Davy, get Storm."

Davy was getting Meg Sarah's tack. He turned to Joanna. "Are you sure, Joanna? Storm is your favorite."

"Ay," Joanna said, taking the bridle from Davy. "Hurry, now. Storm is the fastest horse we have. He will carry Meg Sarah safely through the enemy lines."

Davy nodded, and the two worked together to saddle Storm.

Joanna went to the horse's head and stroked the white moon shape on his forehead. "Go, my beauty," she whispered. "Run, Sirrah. Run like you've never run before. Lucus's life depends on you. And Meg Sarah's. Don't let me down."

Meg Sarah appeared, bag in hand. She saw Storm and darted a questioning glance to Joanna, who nodded in affirmation. Davy gave Meg Sarah a leg up. Joanna placed a hand over her sister's. "Ride hard, Meg. Don't look back." Meg nodded and galloped off.

"May the Master go with thee," Joanna murmured, watching until they were out of sight.

Meg Sarah rode hard through the night. Upon reaching Lucus, she did her best to help him, and the boy did seem to improve slightly under her care. Three days later, however, he took a turn for the worse, and Meg Sarah, fearing he was living his last days, called for all of his siblings to come see their brother before he died.

Joanna could not remember a day in her life when she had cried so much. Now no more tears would come, and she sat without a sound in the tent where her siblings had gathered around Lucus to bid him farewell. The lad had been unconscious, barely breathing at all, for two days. Joanna looked around at her siblings. Meg Sarah's face was drawn and wore a pinched look. She wiped Lucus's face with a cool cloth. Lines under her eyes showed that she had not slept much since she had come to care for Lucus. Juliet sat by Lucus's side, holding his hand, her face streaked with tears and her eyes red. Davy sat by

Lucus's other side. He had not said a word since he had arrived, though Joanna had seen him shed a few tears. Dick sat by the door of the tent, staring blankly into space. He seemed resigned to Lucus's fate. Suddenly Joanna could not stand it any longer. She rose and turned to leave. Meg Sarah looked up at her. "Joanna, where are you going? You only just got here."

"I can't just sit here and watch my brother die," Joanna hissed with more force than she intended.

"Then you will leave us all?" Meg Sarah asked softly.

"The Master must come," Joanna said, excited as the idea came to her. She turned to Meg Sarah. "I must find the Master. He will heal Lucus."

Meg Sarah shook her head sadly. "The Master is not here, Joanna. Beside, if'n the Master was to spare Lucus, He would have done it already," Meg Sarah added, speaking as though gently scolding a disillusioned child. "It is too late, Joanna. It is Lucus's time." Meg Sarah reached out and took Joanna's hand tenderly, but Joanna twisted away and left the tent. She ran blindly through the forest, fresh tears stinging at her eyes. She ran as fast as she could, as if the exertion would somehow abate the anger and frustration and sadness that welled up within her. Her lungs burned and her legs felt like jelly, but she only pushed herself to go faster. Finally she collapsed in a clearing, weeping and gasping for breath. Once the girl had had a good cry and all was silent again except for the twittering of the birds, she became aware of a light touch upon her shoulder.

"Child."

Joanna immediately recognized the gentle voice. "Master," she cried, turning. The Master smiled down at her. "Master, I was looking for You."

"'Tis so? Ay, and all who seek Me shall find Me," quoth He.

"Alack, my Master! My brother, who I love, is sick even unto death. I beseech Thee to come lay Thy hand upon him that he may live."

"Ay, Dearest, let us be off then," said He, taking her hand and helping her up.

So the two began the walk back to the camp. The Master pointed out to Joanna the birds and flowers of that part of the wood that the girl had not taken time to notice before. As the two walked along side-by-side, the Master told her of the creatures and plants and of their ways. Presently they reached the camp, and Joanna, who had momentarily forgotten the urgency of her mission, suddenly remembered Lucus's plight and ran ahead to the tent.

Meg Sarah looked up as Joanna entered. "Joanna--" she began, then the words abruptly died on her lips when she saw the Master. Everyone had gathered around Lucus, and Dick was pulling a cloth over the boy's face.

Joanna let out a strangled cry, and abruptly covered her mouth with her hand.

Meg Sarah spoke softly. "Master, he is dead. It is too late."

The Master said nothing to this, only moved toward Lucus's body, and the four moved back to allow Him space. Kneeling, the Master uncovered the boy's face. The others turned away, out of respect for the dead. The Master moved his fingers over Lucus's forehead and began to murmur a prayer in Latin. The rest finally looked, just in time to see Lucus's blue eyes flicker open. They watched in amazement as the boy blinked a few times, then sat up. Everyone looked to see the Master's expression, but He had vanished as soon as he saw that Lucus was up.

Meg Sarah was the first to move. "His heart stopped beating. There was no pulse. The Master has assuredly raised him," she said in awe, reaching to touch Lucus. Lucus laughed and flinched away. "Meg, I'm not one of your science specimens. Come, why are you all staring at me?"

Juliet flung herself at Lucus and began to laugh and cry at the same time. Davy joined and soon they were all laughing and crying and hugging each other.

Meanwhile, the Iovis had heard that Lucus was dying, and that the Six were all together in one place. They decided to seize the opportunity to take the Six while they were weak. They gathered all their force together and marched on the camp of the Noble Six. But they found the Six armed and waiting for them. What was supposed to be a sneak attack on a small grieving party turned out to be something different altogether. The Iovis were beaten badly and there was such a great slaughter that the Iovis were forced to surrender or there would be no more Iovis.

The Spar-ion War was finally over. However, Dicken had been wounded in the last battle, and one day, Meg Sarah came to Joanna privately.

"I must take Dicken to the sea-shore on the west coast," she said. "The warm sun and the salt air will do him good, and he will have some rest and quiet there to recover of his wounds. Beside, I have heard the

Master is there."

"Ay, you must take him," Joanna agreed. "How long will you be gone?"

"Two moons at the least," Meg Sarah returned.

Joanna looked thoughful. "Ay. Then we will all come also."

"Nay, sister. I will take Dicken. The rest of you must stay," Meg Sarah urged. "There must be some to go out and come in before the subjects. They need a king. We must appoint Lucus to be king in Dick's stead until his return. And he must needs you for his advisor. And the rest of the Iovis must be dealt with."

Joanna sighed and looked out to where the rebuilding of the Royal Mansion had already begun. Lucus had seemingly taken charge of the work. She nodded to Meg. "Do what you think best, sister. I have verily put the king in your charge."

Meg Sarah nodded. "We leave in the morning."

And so early the next morning Meg's group started out. They rather resembled a solemn funeral procession, Joanna thought. Dick was being pulled in a cart in the middle, flanked by his two lions. Meg rode in the lead, followed by all of her servants on horseback, then there was Dick's cart and all Dick's servants followed behind. Joanna was saddened to think that this could be the last time she saw Dicken alive. He might never come back. This could indeed be his funeral procession. She went to the cart to bid Dick goodbye.

The lad was either sleeping or unconscious, his eyes closed and his long dark lashes like black smudges on his white cheeks. Joanna's heart clenched as she observed the deep lines in Dick's young face.

Poor Dicken. The war had been so hard on him. It had aged him so much. Maybe Meg Sarah was right, and he just needed a little peace and quiet. Joanna bent and kissed Dick's forehead. She backed away slowly, murmuring a blessing. Meg Sarah came to speak to Joanna, and the two sisters embraced and held each other for a moment without a word.

"You will send word if there is any change?" said Joanna softly.

"Ay, sister."

Joanna went to join Lucus and Davy as they watched the procession slowly move out.

Upon returning to camp, she saw Juliet packing.

"Where are you going?" Joanna questioned.

"I'm leaving," returned Juliet.

"What? Why?"

"The war is over. I need a sabbatical. Is there a problem with that?"

Joanna sighed. "I suppose not. How long will you be gone?"

"A few months. I will be back for the Court."

Joanna let her mount settle into a loose trot as she moved deeper into the Great Wood. It had been a stressful past few months ruling the land without Dick, and now she needed a few hours of space and fresh air and time alone. Most of her time, to be sure, had been spent watching out for Lucus. The boy had to be kept on a short leash or he was certain to cause trouble. And what with the ongoing construction of the mansion and the nearing Iovis court, there was no room for error. And now neither Juliet nor Meg Sarah was around to keep Lucus in line.

There had been no word from Meg Sarah. Joanna had decided that no news must be good news, then. At least for now. At least she had not heard that Dick had died. Looking up, Joanna saw that the sun was now high in the sky. It was time to head back. She had already been gone too long, and there was work to do.

Joanna was sitting at her desk in the mansion, working on some papers, when Davy came in.

"Davy," Joanna greeted, putting aside her pen so she could give her youngest brother her full attention.

"Joannas, there is a party outside from the east. They claim to have brought aught of yours," Davy said.

Joanna raised her eyebrows. "Ay? Aught of mine, you say? What is it?"

Davy shrugged. "Verily, I wist not. Prithee go see them yourself, for they look to have come a long way to see you and are even now standing in the inner court."

Joanna rose. "Let us not keep them waiting then."

She followed Davy to the court.

The strange assortment of a dozen creatures that stood in the court did indeed appear weary from traveling, as Davy had said. Seeing Joanna, a samanta who appeared to be the leader of the band stepped forward. "Madame Joannas," he said, bowing low, "we have recovered aught of yours." He signaled to the rest, and they stepped back from the creature who stood in the middle of the group.

Davy, who was standing beside Joanna, frowned when he saw the dirty, thin, scarred horse that stood there, head drooping. Joanna had access to thousands of handsome, healthy chargers in the royal stables, yet this party had come all this way to bring her a lame, broken-down old war horse? The forlorn beast suddenly lifted its head and nickered at Joanna. Then it clicked. It seemed to have clicked with Joanna as well. "Storm?" she whispered incredulously, moving forward. Sliding her hand under the dirty, matted mane, she found the familiar white moon shape on the horse's forehead. The stallion whinnied weakly and nudged the girl's shoulder. It was Storm. Joanna hugged the horse's skinny neck happily. Storm had been lost after that night Meg Sarah had galloped him through enemy lines. Joanna had supposed she would never see him again. Now here he was.

Davy shook his head, as if convincing himself that he would never understand girls, and headed off to go back to his own business.

The day of the Iovis court came. Lucus sat on the throne with Joanna by his side and watched as the last of the Iovis slunk in and stood before him to hear their fate. The leader, Jamah, wore a cut robe that showed off his many scars he had acquired during the war. Joanna glances sideways at Lucus. His expression was grim. The decision that lay before him was a difficult one. It was because of the Iovis that Dick was ill. It was because of the Iovis that the Spar-ion war had dragged on so. Joanna could not blame Lucus one bit if he had all the Iovis executed on the spot today. But that was revenge. The Chosen Ones were not supposed to take revenge. The Great One must approve the court here. That is what Dicken would have wanted. Oh that Dicken were here! Dick was so good and wise. He would have known just what to do with the lovis. Now the power lay in Lucus's not-so-capable hands. He was the king.

Lucus looked at the keeper of records, who nodded in answer to his silent question. Yes, all of the lovis were in attendance. Lucus nodded to Joanna to begin the proceedings. She banged the gavel, and there was silence in the court. All eyes went to Lucus, who slowly rose from the throne. He stood silently looking over the lovis for several moments. Juliet, who was standing at the back of the room, noted that Lucus was calmer and more composed than she had ever seen him.

Lucus began. "According unto the power vested in me as acting king of our great land, I hereby declare this court in session and myself as presider in any and all affairs."

He paused, then went on.

"For their traitorous acts against the crown and their warrings thereof, I hereby declare the lovis standing here as guilty before the king and his subjects and before the Great One Himself Who has appointed them."

Joanna pressed her lips together. Yes, the lovis were guilty. That did not have to be decided. But what would their punishment be? Her gaze went to Juliet, and she noted that the girl's eyes were closed, and her lips moved in silent prayer. Davy, who was standing on the other side of

Lucus, was fervently crossing himself.

"Therefore--" Lucus began, then paused to shoot Joanna and Davy a look. The two quickly snapped to attention and did their best to look normal.

"Therefore," Lucus started again, "I hereby banish the Iovis to the Country of Hills."*

Jamah's shoulders slumped. "You doom us," he said gloomily. "Whyk, it is better for us to die here than in the accursed hills. We will starve."

"You will be permitted to bring all your belongings, including grain and seeds. You shall not die of hunger," Lucus said.

Jamah shrugged. "That availeth naught. Alack, we shall be hated above all, and all who see us shall kill us."

"Nay," said Lucus. "But the Iovis in his own place shall be avenged four times over."

So the Iovis left the court, never to be in the presence of a king of Tagawoogah again for many more years.

* The Country of Hills was a hot, barren wasteland spotted with cactus and shrub-brush. The dragons of Tagawoogah used to live there before the Noble Six had hunted them to extinction. The dragons had become numerous during the time of the Black Knight and the Witch, and this unusually large population had eaten the grass and trees down to the roots in the Country of Hills and reduced the lakes and rivers down to tiny pools and trickling streams. Since then, no plants would grow well. Though the Country of Hills was technically part of Tagawoogah, it was near the border and not under the protection of the king. King Richard

had ruled long ago that hunting was allowed in the Country of Hills, though it was not allowed in Tagawoogah. The Iovis would be forced to spend all their waking hours digging for roots, scouting for water, and laboring in their gardens to grow a few plants so they could survive.

"So I am very proud of Lucus," Joanna added as she finished telling Storm what had happened during the Iovis court and subsequent journey to see the Iovis and their belongings safely to the Country of Hills. "Now all of us shall be rid of the quarrelsome Iovis, who now shall be too busy gathering food to pick any fights. And there was no additional shedding of blood on our part." She ran her brush once more over Storm's side, then stepped back to see the results of her work.

It had been a few months since Storm had been brought to the mansion, and Joanna had been able to nurse the horse back to health. His ribs no longer showed, and his mane and coat now exhibited some of their former shine. But nothing could cure his lameness. No longer was Storm fit to carry a rider in war or on long rides across the country. But Joanna was determined to care for the horse until the end. Suddenly a shrill whistle pierced the early morning air. It was the herd of wild horses that had been regularly passing the Royal Mansion in their rounds. Joanna watched Storm. His small, pointed ears were pricked up and he had moved closer to the window, watching the herd. "You do not want to go with them, Storm," she said gently, "You will not be able to keep up with them." But Storm did want to go. Joanna patted her horse's neck and looked into his eyes. Yes, it was time for the faithful horse to retire. To live the rest of his days wild and free. Slowly she opened the door to the stall and led Storm outside. The wild horses whinnied to Storm, and Storm held his head high and whinnied back. She led him to the edge of the grounds and outside the gate where she paused to stroke his soft nose. Then she reached up and gently slid off his halter. Storm tossed his head and trotted to join the herd. Joanna moved back against the fence and watched as the other horses greeted Storm.

Joanna felt a hand on her shoulder, and she turned to see Dicken grinning down at her. Meg Sarah stood close behind with Davy, Juliet, and Lucus. Joanna reached up to cover Dick's hand with hers. Her eyes shone with tears.

All Six stood together along the fence watching Storm and the wild horses. They were silent, for there were no words that could contain the depth of the emotion of the moment.

THE END

www.ingramcontent.com/pod-product-compliance
Lightning Source LLC
Chambersburg PA
CBHW030149200626
46812CB00016B/1765